FROM YOUR [illegible]

"YOU SA[illegible]!

I'VE NOT [illegible] YET,

BUT IT LOOKED REALLY

INTERESTING. I HOPE YOU LIKE IT!"

MW00681682

MAN AGAINST THE FUTURE

Copyright © 2011 by Bryan Young

Cover design by Lucas and Heather Ackley
www.ackleydesign.com
Book design by Bryan Young
bryan@bigshinyrobot.com

Special Thanks to Dawn Boardman

All rights reserved.
No part of this book may be reproduced in any form or by any electronic or mechanical means including information storage and retrieval systems, without permission in writing from the author. The only exception is by a reviewer, who may quote short excerpts in a review.

Printed in the United States of America
First Printing: June 2011
ISBN-13: 978-0615489506

This is a work of fiction. Names, characters, places, and incidents either are the product of the author's imagination or used fictitiously, and any resemblance to actual persons, living or dead, businesses, companies, events, or locales is entirely coincidental.

To my girls, my son, and all the rest of you who supported me through the best and worst of my days writing these stories.

To everyone else, I hope you enjoy them anyway.

-BY 2011

MAN AGAINST THE FUTURE

The Hope of Humanity

The year was 2081 and so many of the social problems humans had faced over the last hundred years were still a pretty big problem. Most people were still poor, corporations still ran the government, and politicians were constantly caught with prostitutes of both sexes, living and dead. When politicians weren't blowing each other's personal lives completely out of proportion for political gain, they were starting wars with other countries. Sometimes, they would even start wars with people inside their own country, but those were usually ideological. Perhaps the biggest and worst change was that the polar ice caps had melted and much of the Mojave Desert was now prime beachfront property. That, and the air across the globe tasted like you were sucking on a tailpipe.

As pressing and horrible as those issues were, they really didn't enter into the minds of John and Mildred Bates. They were working class and average in most ways. John worked a standard sixty hour work week and, to help make ends meet, Mildred picked up thirty-nine hours a week, part time, working at the deli counter at the local, national chain grocery emporium.

Even with all those hours, supporting their modest household and single child, John, Jr., was a difficult exercise. After the mortgage, the bills, the poor tax, and their basic needs, there wasn't a lot left over for leisure, though they had saved up their pennies for quite a while to afford the sizable HD television which was the centerpiece for their living space.

Each night after work, John Bates would settle into his favorite tattered easy chair, that he still made regular payments on, crack open an ice cold beer, and watch his immense television. Despite his disinterest, he liked to watch the local, nationally syndicated-for-the-region news. Little John, Jr., just before bedtime, would sit cross-legged in the space of carpet between his father and the television, transfixed by every image shown on the high definition display.

"Tonight, we have a special live program for you from science reporter Kurt Sanders."

"Mildred! Can you grab another beer for me, love?"

The Hope of Humanity

"This is Kurt Sanders, and I'm here at the Monsanto Space Center in Cape Canaveral, Florida, reporting live for a momentous occasion, both for science and for mankind."

"Yes, dear! I'll grab another can from the ice box."

"With me, I have Doctor Thaddeus Quentin, chief architect of Project: Humanity, brought to you by Exxon, which is launching in a rocket in T-minus eight minutes."

Mildred arrived a moment later in the living room with John's beer, putting it in his hand and leaning down, pulling the foot rest on his recliner up for him. He sipped the head of the beer that had flowed over the lip of the can, paying far less attention to the launch than his boy was.

"What we're doing is really quite simple. The top minds in the world have created a sixty year plan to fix the problems of the world. Everything that ails us: hunger, disease, war, and so forth, and they've committed to monetizing those solutions for their sponsors..."

John, Jr., blinked. At seven years old these concepts were still just a bit too abstract for his innocent little mind. He'd been hungry before, but he couldn't understand how it could be a problem since food seemed so readily available. And he didn't think disease would have been a big deal because whenever he got too sick, he would be taken to the emergency room. And war was something cool that his dad had showed him in movies. But he was appropriately naïve for his age, like all boys his age should be.

"What we're doing is quite revolutionary in order to solve the mortality problem and allow these brilliant minds and captains of industry to oversee their plan to the end and beyond."

John slurped his beer, worn to the bone. Mildred listened to the broadcast from the kitchen where the smells of a cooking dinner were all consuming.

"...and could you explain to our audience at home how you plan to conquer 'the mortality problem?'"

"Time travel," the good doctor said as he flashed a sparkling grin at the camera.

At the sound of the phrase, little Junior's eyes widened and his ears perked up. This was the sort of television that fired the imaginations of little boys the world over into overdrive.

"Time travel? How is that possible?"

"By going very far, very fast. We're going to blast them into space and they're going to approach the speed of light on their way out of our solar system and galaxy. Then they'll sling shot back. The closer to the speed of light they travel, the faster time on Earth goes by. It's the time dilation effect. Their voyage will take about ten years for them, but we estimate about sixty years will have elapsed on Earth by the time they come back."

Junior's eyes were as wide as saucers and the hairs on his neck were raised on end. "Dad, dad..." the boy turned to his father, excited. "They're flying to the future!"

"Eh?" The older John looked up, noticing the flashing images on the screen as Dr. Quentin introduced the audience at home to the rocket ship's crew, the Earth's first recorded Time Travelers. The Captain, the crew, the science team, the business leaders, the support crew, all the families, there were a hundred and four in all.

"Each of them are heroes of the highest order, embarking on this ten year odyssey in the name of science, of profit, and in the name of humanity."

Dr. Quentin cut in, taking the microphone from the reporter, "Make no doubts about it, Kurt, we are sending Earth's most brilliant minds as a gift to the future."

"And here we are, with one minute left. You can see on your television the enormity of the rocket--"

"--it has to be that big, Kurt, in order to facilitate the nuclear blasts required to achieve near-speed-of-light travel."

Both John and his son were completely entranced by the screen with a burning sensation of pride in their chest. This was what humanity could achieve if we worked together.

"All our problems will be solved then, won't they son?"

John, Jr., could only nod; his eyes could not leave the screen.

"While they're gone, they'll have a crew of ten working in the greenhouse on board, making sure the ship is well supplied with oxygen and fresh food for all hands on deck."

"Do they have any livestock on board, Doctor?"

"Of course, they had access to some of thc last remaining livestock resources on our planet. There will be very little reprocessing for them, the ship was designed to be completely sustainable on their voyage."

John, Sr. took long, deep gulps of his beer, paying an unusual amount of attention to the television.

"And why is it they decided to bring their families along, Doctor?"

"I think that's rather obvious, Kurt. They'll be gone for sixty of our Earth years. When they come back, they'll be able to carry on their family lives as though they haven't missed a beat. They won't return to be younger than their grandchildren."

"Are we sure this will work, Doctor? I mean, time travel sounds a bit far fetched..."

"The science is sound, Kurt. The consensus of the scientific community is that this will work. And I've seen the data and everything suggests complete success."

Without realizing it, John, Jr., had been inching closer and closer to the television. In fact, he'd gotten so close that the letter boxed screen encompassed the entirety of his field of vision. He was at a rapt state of complete attention.

"Why aren't you going along, Dr. Quentin?"

"Well, we decided to hold one mind here in reserve on Earth, to shepherd the project along while they are gone on their momentous voyage. There is a lot to do in the next sixty years if we're going to fix the world, and their work needs to carry on. They've given me the blueprint and I hope to get things off the ground before my time is up. I'll pass the torch to others beyond me, and they'll pass that torch along until these brilliant minds return."

"Fascinating, Doctor. You really are onto something important here, sir."

"I sure hope so. We're really putting all our eggs into one basket, so to speak."

As the countdown to the launch began, neither John, Sr., nor his son, realized they were holding their breath.

"Now, with thirty seconds left, we're about to witness the launch of the fastest, most immense ship ever fired into the outer-reaches of space."

"With twenty-five seconds left, I'm reminding myself that this is a moment we will all remember in the collective memory of society for years to come, like the first time we walked on the moon, or the September 11 attacks, or the annexation of Mexico."

"Indeed, and it's important to remind the audience that this is the first time humans will have left our galaxy. But now we're about to go to the countdown at mission control."

"This is mission control. We have launch in T-minus ten.

"Nine.

"Eight.

"Seven.

"Six.

"Five.

"Four.

"Three.

"Two.

"One. We have lift off."

In a brilliant flash of light and accompanied by the sound of rolling thunder, The Hope of Humanity was launched into space, hurtling toward the heavens.

"And there it is. The Hope of Humanity has launched. It's a beautiful sight. The rocket and all of its crew are just a few seconds from leaving the Earth's atmosphere, not to return for another sixty years."

And that's when something went wrong.

With the eyes of the world watching, the rocket exploded into a fiery ball of shorn, metal debris, killing anyone and anything inside.

The television feed cut back to the reporters, horrified looks nestled firmly on their faces. "Uhh... Ladies and gentlemen, it seems as though... this is a terrible, terrible tragedy... The rocket has exploded, everyone inside is most likely dead. The hope of the future exploded just before it left the Earth's atmosphere."

While Kurt and his colleagues struggled to swallow their tears and find words to describe the catastrophe that occurred on live television, little John, Jr., burst into deep, troubled sobs, trying hard to comprehend what he just saw. A shivering thrill of excitement had run up his back, only to turn to tears and terror instantly.

He stood up and ran to the loving arms of his mother who walked into the room, wondering what the commotion was about.

"What happened?" she asked as she put her arms around her son while he cried into her apron.

For all the gruffness of his exterior, John was having a hard time holding back tears. "The space ship... It exploded..."

"Oh, dear," she said. The blood ran from her face as she realized that more than a hundred of the world's brightest minds were lost in that single moment.

John couldn't bear going to work the next day and neither could Mildred. John, Jr. stayed home from school. The entire world was in a state of shock and no one was faulted for closing their businesses for the day and curling up in the fetal position in front of their televisions, hoping to find some sense in such a senseless event.

For days and weeks and months and years after, pundits, scientists, and anyone in between would debate the cause of the explosion on TV, the news, and the internet, but the answer was pretty simple: That's just what happens when you live in a world without meaningful regulations and is run by force of profit motive: the lowest bidder always wins the contracts.

Hatchet

It had been a full night and most of a day since we'd been trapped in the basement of my mother's house. There was one door leading up and out, and bars over windows too small to escape from.

We had to barricade our one escape route to keep my mother and sister out.

"I don't know long we'll be able to stay here." Leave it to my little brother to state the obvious.

"I know. But what else can we do?"

"I don't know."

I shouldn't have come here. He called me and asked me to come check on our mother and sister. They'd come home from a shopping trip with a fever that put them both down in bed with a vengeance.

"They're not responsive. I know you're busy, but I want to know if you think I should take them to a doctor."

Without observing them firsthand I could tell they needed to see a doctor, but I think my little brother needed me more than they did. I could hear it in his voice. It wasn't long after I came over that everything went to hell. Whatever infection they'd contracted gave them a bloodlust that made them kill our middle brother and forced us to take refuge in the basement with our five-year-old sister.

For the last twelve hours we'd been through a sleepless night, trying to come up with a plan in an unfinished basement with a constant banging and rattling on the door. We knew the gurgling and screaming was what was left of our loved ones, but that only made it that much more unsettling.

Everything had gone down so fast that I'm not even clear about what had occurred. I know if I had to do it all again, I certainly wouldn't have left my cell phone in the car. There were no means of communication in the basement, in or out. No TV. No phone. Nothing. We had no way of knowing how widespread this was. I had no idea how to call my wife and children to make sure they were okay. I had no way to do much of anything.

My best guess was that this fever hit a lot of people; otherwise my wife would have sent the police here to bail us out. But who knows?

On the plus side, we had plenty of food and water if it came to that. The food storage and water heater were secure in the basement. My mind had come up with plenty of long term survival ideas (for example, we could cook with an open flame on the concrete floor as long as we were careful and the windows were cracked to let out the smoke), but I wanted to get out of there as soon as I possibly could.

I also had a hatchet. It was a holdover from a campout my Dad had taken us on when he was still around. It was rusted and had spent the last two decades in a tool box next to the furnace.

The hardest part was reassuring Leigh, our five year old sister, that everything was going to be okay. Thankfully, she was sleeping at the moment. The time she was awake was spent going through boxes of old family photos and wondering out loud what had happened to her mother.

Anthony checked Leigh once more and put a blanket on her, an old cotton one from my childhood with E.T. and Elliot on it. Then he came over to me, sat down, and wondered aloud what we were going to do.

"You know what we have to do."

"You really think no one's coming?"

"I have no idea. But I'm sure someone would have come by now."

"It's only been since yesterday."

"I know. I think if anyone was coming it would have happened by now."

"Then why are we still here?"

"I don't know. I'm going crazy. I haven't even talked to Jenny or the kids since before I came here, since before all this..."

"You really think this is happening everywhere?"

"I can't think of any other reason why no one has come to help us."

"And you really think...?"

"Yes, Tony. I do. Will you stop asking me questions? You've seen as many movies that start like this as I have."

"So you don't think there's another way?"

"No."

"I can't do it."

"You think I can?"

We'd had the same argument over and over again for the last few hours. He couldn't do what needed to happen. Obviously Leigh couldn't. It was clear: if I ever wanted to get to my wife and children and have my remaining siblings survive, I was going have to do it myself; I would have to bludgeon what was left of my mother and sister to death with a dull hatchet.

I alternated between finding the resolve to do it and wanting to wait it out because I wasn't sure if I was capable of the violence the situation required.

"How long do you think they'll keep on that door?"

"I don't know, Anthony. I have no idea. I have no answers. You know as much as I do."

On cue, the scratching at the door grew louder. I looked up the stairway and tried to remember times I had down here that were less horrific...

...Reading a comic book atop that old bean bag, only to be interrupted by my mother's call to dinner...

...Building forts with my brother on either side of the room for our action figures...

...Skipping school with friends and sneaking down here to play Mario Kart on the old big screen we used to have down here...

Perhaps the most poignant and sweet memory of this basement was sneaking down here with my wife before we were married and making love, silently in the dark.

All of those memories and a hundred more would be shattered into tiny pieces. After the end of this ordeal, it would all be eclipsed by this terror. It would turn all of my memories here into a horror film.

In the end, it wouldn't be a choice at all. If I wanted to get my brother and baby sister out of this, if I ever wanted to see my wife and infant children again, I would have to find the strength.

Never in my wildest imagination did I ever dream that my life would depend on my ability to warm up to the idea of chopping my beloved mother and little sister into hamburger with an axe.

"And you won't?"

Vehemently, Anthony shook his head. He was always much more of a momma's boy than I was. It was no surprise that he'd leave me to do the dirty work.

It was then that the scratching at the door stopped. Anthony and I shared a scared look and listened hard to find a clue as to what was going on.

"Maybe they collapsed," Anthony whispered to me.

I shrugged.

Knowing full well he wouldn't volunteer, and forcing him to do it would be the same thing as sending him to his death, I hefted the hatchet, taking on the responsibility myself. "I'll go first. You grab Leigh and stay close behind. If there's a problem, I'll take care of it, but you get to my car."

I handed him the keys.

"Okay."

"You get her in the car and you wait for me."

He seemed in shock. He knew what was coming.

"Anthony?"

He took a breath and finally nodded his head in the affirmative. I could only imagine what was running through his mind. None of it was pretty.

"It's just like that aliens game we used to play with the foam guns."

Anthony scooped Leigh up in his arms, stirring her awake. "What's going on?"

I kissed her on the forehead, "We're leaving, sweetie."

Looking down, I considered the axe in my hand and looked back to Leigh, and then to Anthony, "You keep her eyes covered."

He nodded again.

"We have everything we need?"

Once more he nodded.

I paused to give them both a hug, to bolster their strength and mine.

With that, I took the lead, creeping slowly up the stairs as quietly as possible. Anthony, Leigh heavy in his arms behind me, did the same.

As quietly as I could, I pulled the boards we'd used to barricade the door and lay them down on the stairs. Each squeak and squawk of a nail or the wood giving made my hair raise, my teeth clench, and my blood boil. Once the boards were removed, I delicately put my ear to the door, trying hard to hear what might be happening on the other side.

It was of no use.

We'd be going into this situation blind. How could we be sure our family members were still even out there? What if some other band of wandering undead stumbled into our house and...and...?

I was grasping at straws. I didn't want my mother or my sister to be out there. It was just wishful thinking. If it were strangers behind that door, there wouldn't be any issue and my heart would not be so heavy. Bludgeoning an anonymous zombie would be infinitely easier than what I was likely to face.

Behind the door was dark. It was twilight outside and the different swaths of orange and blue light painted the living room with an eerie glow. The only thing more unsettling than the light was the lack of sound. It was as though the world was on mute.

Anthony crept up behind me, Leigh in his arms, staying close.

Step after careful step we came out into a room we'd both spent too much time in, watching television, playing games, spending family time together...

But now everything was dead quiet.

I knew there was something wrong when I felt my foot slip beneath me. I'd stepped into a puddle of thick tar that I realized was a collection of infected, coagulated blood the color of midnight. Reducing my voice to a whisper, I pointed down at the mess and told Anthony to watch out.

Leading away from the sludge was a trail of the dark liquid, heading in the direction of the front door. "I think they're gone. Let's get to the car."

Each step we took toward the door doubled the anxiety welling in my stomach. Every bit of me wanted to cry and be done with all of this all at the same time.

At long last, we reached the threshold of the front door and I turned the knob, pulling the door open.

The car was there, just like I'd left it, but that didn't matter because there was a horrible screeching and gurgling coming from the kitchen and heading our way fast...

I shoved Anthony and Leigh out the door toward the car. "Go!"

I turned around and blocked the doorway with my body. What was left of my mother and sister wouldn't get to what was left of my family without killing me to do it.

Seeing them was harder than I thought it would be. Huge chunks of their hair was missing, their mouths were oozing the thick blood like drool. I couldn't be sure if it was their blood or if they'd eaten some other rotted thing. They limped and hobbled toward me just like you'd expect them to. Their eyes were a pale, milky white all the way through and all the love they once held was gone.

Their pace quickened and the noises they made grew louder. It was low in the throat, like the growl of a cat.

I decided I didn't want to be around for much longer so I made a dash for the car.

Anthony had made it inside with Leigh, but had locked the doors. I pulled up on the handle at the same time he tried unlocking the door for me twice in a row, dooming me to my fate.

"Open the fucking door!"

The cat growling had grown into screeching and they were directly behind me. I couldn't open the door to the car while they were this close and risk exposing the others.

The axe must have weighed a hundred pounds at that moment.

Knowing I had to do it, I tried to banish every thought of love and caring I'd ever had for my mother and sister. My only chance was to summon every ounce of hate and loathing that I could muster.

But I loved them. Hate and loathing were not something I had just laying around for these people.

By this time, I'm sure I must have been crying like a baby.

The blade went into my sister's temple and all I could think of was all the times she tattled on me as a child, but it wasn't good enough.

I needed something worse than that.

My sister fell backward but recovered quickly, without missing a beat.

Her hands were raised, coming for me, I tried to dodge and the hatchet connected with her neck limply. The rage I could muster was in trade for all the times I'd been grounded on her account.

But it wasn't enough.

Her forward momentum brought her careening onto the car where Leigh was seeing this, shrieking and crying like any five year old in this situation would be expected to do. Anthony tried his hardest to shush her and cover her eyes, but she was hysterical.

I found the anger to finish my sister by the fury of what I'd been forced to do. I connected the full force of the axe into her forehead, cleaving her head in two. She dropped to the ground, down for the count. I hoped, anyway.

My mother and I turned for each other and I hit her with every bit of hurt I could muster for every embarrassment I ever suffered at her hands.

But she still kept at me.

Once more I hit her. Finally, I got her in the bloody, flailing arm. This time, it was with the anguish I felt when I thought of losing her.

But it wasn't enough.

I had to reach. Deep down. There was something still holding me back, but then it came... Like a flood, washing over me, letting it all go.

I hit her with the pain I felt every time I watched her do nothing when my father would attack me senselessly, viciously, before she left him.

With the force of every injury she ever watched him inflict upon me I smashed the axe through her. And again. And again and again and again.

I was a wild animal. A caged jungle cat who'd finally been let free and lashed out at the keeper keeping him.

It wasn't until I looked up to see Anthony and Leigh crying, still locked in the car, that I thought to stop. My hands were covered in the thick tar to my forearms and my face was bleeding tears.

"I'm sorry," I said aloud, softly. "I'm sorry."

Like a fool, I dropped the axe and was able to get into the car and Anthony floored it.

Leigh crawled into my lap. I held her and we cried and cried and cried.

It would have been an understatement to say that this might have been the worst day of my life. But things would get better when I found my wife and children safe...

They'd have to, right?

An Original

Her back was turned to him and she couldn't see her husband when he came in. She couldn't see that he was bleeding in half a dozen places, bruised and battered, grass stains on his clothes. The sounds of his panting, though, were enough to turn her attention toward him.

She gasped when she saw the state of him, but didn't have time to ask what was wrong.

He began for her: "Do you love me?"

"Of course."

"Really? No matter what's happens?"

She pulled a bit of the shrubbery from his hair and gently put her hand on his face, trying her hardest to reassure him. "Of course I love you. Nothing could ever change that."

"I hope so," he said as he collapsed into a chair, fighting back tears.

"What's wrong?" Her voice quivered with concern.

"What if I told you something..." He could barely continue. "Something about me. And it would change everything. Would you still love me?"

"Will you please just tell me what happened?"

"I'm serious. Will things change?"

"How can I know that if you won't tell me what the problem is?"

"It's not so easy, and I'm not all that sure..." He stopped, trying to catch his breath. "It's all so much of a shock, I don't even know what..."

With a quiet, loving tone, she shushed him, trying her hardest to calm him. He was shaking beneath her touch.

"Just tell me what the matter is," she whispered delicately in his ear, "and I promise that it'll all be okay."

He looked up at her, took a breath, and--

"Please, take a seat, Mr. Drake," his attorney said, graciously motioning toward a plush leather chair opposite his desk. Steven Drake settled into the chair and folded his legs, assuming this all had something to do with his parents' will. The lawyer sat down in his chair with a creak, both of his back and the mechanical swivel under his seat. The lawyer was a very young partner for his profession, about the same age as Steven. Both men were in their early thirties and neither showed signs of graying. "Do you know why I asked you here today?"

"I imagine it has something to do with some dangling legal threads from the passing of my parents."

"That was tragic. Yes, it does, have something to do with that. Once again, I am deeply sorry for the loss of your parents."

"Thank you. It was terrible, but I think they'd be the first to say that they both led full lives with no regrets."

"You never know, Steven. Sometimes, you really never know."

"I suppose not," he said as he picked a spot of lint from his slacks.

"Well, technically, this is a matter that stems from your parents untimely loss."

"I just figured that since we'd been through the will this would have been all taken care of by now."

"Well, this matter is a little more complicated than that, unfortunately."

Steven furrowed his brow, curious, "What's the matter then?"

"Would you like a drink?" The attorney pulled a crystal decanter and a pair of scotch glasses from a shelf below the level of the desk and quickly poured two fingers of Scotch for each of them. In the last two years of being a client of John Lindh's, Steven had never been offered a drink inside the sanctum of his office. Something was the matter and it aroused his suspicions and raised the hairs on his neck.

Despite that, he accepted the drink, reaching over and sniffing the beverage. An oakey musk filled his nostrils, he sipped it, and the taste matched the oak bouquet. It went down smooth, warming him on its way. John sniffed and sipped as well, "It's an eighteen year. Oak aged."

"It's very good. But you didn't call me here for this."

"No," he said with a heaving breath. "No, I suppose I didn't."

"I'm grateful for the scotch, but I have to admit that I'm incredibly curious about our purpose here, now."

John stood and turned to face the immense picture window, staring out at the view through the open slats in the wooden Venetian blinds between measured sips of his drink. "This isn't easy for me, but it's not a thing I'm very well equipped to deal with. I'm a lawyer. Breaking news outside of a courtroom isn't my forte, unfortunately."

Steven gave a half chuckle meant to disarm, "I'm a big boy, John. I think I can take it."

John turned his back around, set his glass down on the cherry wood desk and withdrew an aged and battered manila envelope from his filing cabinet. He slid it across the desk to Steven and watched him open it. Steven unwound the string around the front, pulled open the flap, and withdrew a single sheet of paper that had been tapped out on a typewriter. There was no letterhead to speak of and no indication who it was from at first glance, so Steven simply began reading. As he read, his attorney shot down the rest of his scotch, hoping to ease his nerves.

Steven Drake read over the letter, got to the end, and began again. He read the letter again, twice more, before he looked up from his paper and scoffed, "Is this a joke?"

"I wish it was."

Steven's jaw dropped in shock and disbelief. Craning his neck, he drained the rest of his booze, put the empty glass on the desk, and hung his head. "What exactly is this supposed to mean?"

"As your attorney, it means a lot more than I think it should, but the ramifications are... Well, there's...hmmm."

"That's great. The great John Lindh at a loss for words." It was ironic, as young as he was, John Lindh was renowned for his ability to talk his way out of anything inside the courtroom. "You can't be serious. There's no way. If this were true, I'd have known about it."

"Believe it. They left all the evidence in the safe deposit box anyone could ask for. If the letter and I can't convince you, there's files and files. It's true, without a doubt. Trust me. I went over it all myself, twice. It all checks out. Believe me. It all checks out."

"You're seriously telling me that I'm a clone?"

"I'm afraid so."

Steven's world shrunk. At that moment, his eyes could focus on nothing specific and his ears could hear nothing but the thumping beat of his own heart.

"Hey," John snapped his fingers, "Hey. You awake? Please don't go into shock on me, Steven." But Steven couldn't hear him. "I don't want to alarm you, Steven, but things are a little worse than that."

The saliva evaporated in Steven's mouth as the hearing was slowly restored to his ears. "How?" He coughed. "How could it get worse?"

"Well, this conversation isn't covered under the attorney-client privilege of confidentiality."

John was positive no more blood could drain from Steven's face, making him pale even further, but there was still yet blood to drain. "How so?"

"Well, not many of people know the finer details of the Bioethics and Anti-Cloning legislation, but buried in it is a little clause that completely tied my hands in this matter."

"What clause? What do you mean your hands are tied?" Steven asked through another shocked, dry cough.

"It basically supersedes any confidentiality contracts, implied, written or otherwise. It specifically cites an override on attorney client privilege and it compels me to turn you over to the authorities immediately under penalty of a class A felony, punishable by up to a $1 million fine and up to four years in prison."

"What are you saying?"

"What I'm saying is that I like you, and I'm sorry this had to happen. But honestly, neither I nor my firm can incur any risk of lawsuit or federal penalties on your behalf."

"So you're turning me in?"

"I had no choice."

"How long do I have?"

"Not long."

"How long?"

"They arrived right before you did. I'm sorry."

Steven received a jolt of adrenaline and it coursed through his veins. He was suddenly a caged lion, not knowing if he should stay to fight or flee expeditiously.

"I'm sorry," John repeated as the door clicked open and the men in white suits entered aggressively.

That's the moment Steven snapped.

Everything he'd been through in the last ten minutes was so overwhelming that the rational portions of his brain shut off and an animal instinct took over. Rage and betrayal frothed over the brim of his chest and he knew that he wouldn't let these men lay a finger on him while he had a choice. As he weighed that thought against the desire to strangle his former attorney, he barely realized that the glass shattering around him was caused not by some brutal attack on his person, but by his body crashing through the second story office window that John had spent so much time staring out of during their conversation.

Steven hit the shrubbery on the ground floor, hard. It broke his fall, but not enough to prevent him from injuring his right leg. But he was no longer running on corporeal concerns like pain and injuries, but on instinct and base emotion.

Run.

Get away.

Those three words kept repeating in his brain, over and over and over. It was so all-consuming that he didn't even look back to see if the men in white had given chase.

He left his vehicle in the underground structure, beneath the law office headquarters. Not so much because he realized that he would have been stepping into a trap, but because his instincts had put him on his feet and picked a direction.

That's how he made it home, hopping fences, dodging people, sneaking around at a full sprint.

"--and you ran all the way here to ask me if I would still love you?"

"I had to know."

She lowered her head and he couldn't tell from her reaction which side of the fence she would fall on. Carefully, she sighed, confusing him even further. The rage and betrayal from before had slowly turned into simple, raw emotion that boiled up into his eyes and tear ducts, spilling his feelings out in hot, salty streams down his cheeks. After a moment of his involuntary tears, she took a deep breath into her lungs and held it in until she was ready to speak. "I suppose I'm wondering why you even had to ask me."

He blinked and swallowed hard, waiting for her to continue, not yet comprehending her feelings or intentions.

"I love you. And just because you found out that you're not an original, why would that change anything? I'm not in love with the source of your genetic code, I'm in love with you."

He collapsed to his knees, letting the relief wash over him like the surf.

"So what's next? Where do we go from here?"

"I can't ask you to come with me. I need to get out of here. They're after me, there's no sense in getting you involved."

"With all due respect, I said I would be with you no matter what when we got married. This doesn't change anything."

"You'll come with me?"

"I love you. I don't have much a choice."

He grabbed her, pulled her close to him and kissed her. Deeply, passionately, loving her as much as the day he married her.

Then sense took back over, "Then we have to run. Now."

A Pistol Full of Silver

Predictably, the moon was full and set high in the crisp autumn sky on the night I found my family murdered, mutilated, and torn to pieces. Something had crashed through the front window and began to tear them apart one by one. The gas lamps were out, snuffed by the drafty gale rushing in through the shattered window. I entered my home hurriedly, kicking the door open with my boot, illuminating the front room with my lantern. Shadows grew long and flickered in the lamp's firelight. It was the remains of my wife I saw first. I was grateful that the light was so poor because the carnage was too great for me to bear.

A low creak in the wood up the stairs snapped my attention in that direction. I felt a cold rush as the blood drained away from my skin. I must have been pale from fear, but with that fear, my resolve grew. I raised my pistol up to my hip, leveling it toward the noise. I hoped and prayed that it wasn't necessary to have smelted the six silver bullets that occupied each chamber of my revolver, but if they were indeed required to rid the world of this monster, then, by God, I would be prepared. Aiming the light as best I could toward the stairs, I took slow, careful steps in that direction. Another SNAP and a KLUNK stopped me in my tracks. I wished so badly to stop, to turn around to leave this problem to someone else, someone much braver than I, but I knew that wasn't possible. Choking down my fear, I gulped hard and took another step forward.

And another.

And another.

One foot in front of the other, each one in front of the next. Each step closer to the stairs got my heart racing faster. Each step I took up the staircase raised my pulse to match my ascent. I'd worried so much about getting to the stairs and up them that I almost didn't notice the remains of my daughter intermingled with what was left of my wife's body. I didn't realize that hot, salty tears had been streaming from my eyes. It was a completely automatic response; I had to put my grief out of my conscious mind until I'd dispatched this grievous creature.

Finally, I'd reached the top of the stairs, either by overcoming my fear or being overcome by it. I couldn't tell which. Keeping the lantern raised in my left hand and the pistol aimed ahead in my right, I swiveled back and forth, looking for a sign of which hallway to direct my search.

I scanned the floor for any clue or indication, a bloody paw print, a scrap of flesh, anything that could give me an edge. I'd need any and every advantage I could obtain in order to get the drop on the monster. Unfortunately, no sign presented itself, so I stopped, trying my hardest to listen carefully for any audible giveaway. Sadly, I was winded and so severely in fright, that all I could hear was the wheeze of my own labored breathing and a rattle deep in my chest. It was obvious I was just going to have to simply pick a direction in hopes that my instincts proved accurate. My mind raced through worst case scenarios and it flashed instantly to my young boy, aged eight years old. It would make a grim sort of sense that the beast would come up the stairs hoping for an easy snack to go with the main course he'd made of the rest of my family downstairs. With that in my mind, I turned to the left, down the corridor where my son's room resided.

The lantern light swung back and forth down the hallway as I used that arm to wipe the sweat and tears from my brow and cheek.

Down the hall, I could see the door to my boy's bedroom was ajar. No sign of light could be seen through the sliver of bedroom between the door and the jam, only the black of night. This made me nervous. Still, I could hear little but the rusty creaks of the lantern shaking in my fist and my belabored respiration. I crept forward, praying both that I'd guessed right and that my son had hidden away, out of reach of the jaws and claws of the feral beast. I counted slowly to myself, down from three, working hard to compress and contain my overwhelming sense of dread. As I got to the end of my countdown, I was forced to banish all the cowardice I could from my mind and body and quickly nudge the door open with my pistol arm.

And behind the door, there he was!

I caught only a glimpse of him, his head snapped around, his blood red eyes took me in. His snout full of sharp teeth snarled at me, the low growl he emitted was interrupted only by the loud report of my pistol as I squeezed off two quick shots, each missing its mark. Sensing the danger, the bipedal wolf turned quickly away from me and leapt desperately through the second story window, scattering glass across the lawn and shrubs beneath him. Following to the window, I caught sight of him, hitting the earth on all fours, scrambling into the deep thicket that surrounded my once peaceful and lovely country home.

"Damn!" I shouted before I turned, wondering at the ultimate fate of my son. "Jonathon," I called out to him.

No response.

"Jonathon?" I called out once more, to no reply.

I took a glance around the room, pointing at dark corners with my lamp and seeing nothing, neither my boy, nor what could be his desecrated remains. I could not decide if I should have been more worried or relieved when I heard a stirring from the closet. A hopeful sign, to be certain, but I still had to be cautious. I set the lantern on the bureau and watched my shadow shrink further and further as I got closer and closer to the closet door, my hand wavering over the door's knob, aiming my silver loaded gun chest-high toward the closet. With a whoosh, I swung the door open violently to see my boy standing amidst the clothes and various linens. The blood had left his face and he was a clutching a kitchen knife longer than his forearm. Upon the opening of the door, he lunged at me with the serrated instrument. It was fortunate that instead of firing one of the few precious silver bullets left at the boy, I sidestepped and grabbed his wrist, forcing the knife from his grasp. As the knife fell, realization hit him and he understood his father was there. God willing, I'd be able to protect him. By God I'd do my best.

"It got mother," was the only thing the boy could eek out in his stupor of deep shock.

"It's all right, my boy," I assured him, "I'll take care of him. I'll kill him dead."

I clutched the boy to my chest, holding him close, rough but tenderly. He was the dearest possession left to me in this world and I wished that I could have stayed longer to comfort him. But I had to give chase to the beast once more. "Stay here," I told my dear boy, "hide in the wardrobe, stay there until I come to get you."

The boy nodded his understanding.

"If you don't hear from me, do not leave until the morning light. Do you understand?"

The boy said nothing as I guided him back to the mess of cloth. "Do you understand?" I repeated. I had to be sure he comprehended the danger he was in.

"Yes, father," he said meekly.

He sat in the closet, retrieved his knife and looked up at me. His face was sad, void of colour and any other shade of emotion. As I closed the door on him, I told him things would be all right and I silently hoped that this wouldn't be the last time he ever saw his father alive.

With that, I shut him back into what I prayed would not become his tomb and raced down the stairs, then out the door of my home.

The woods seemed dead, the evening breeze had given way to the still of night and it made my spine shiver and the hairs on the back of my neck stand on their end. Once again, I began by creeping slowly in the direction I last saw the monstrosity heading. From the boy's window, he seemed to be heading due East, the direction the sun would be coming from and end him if I couldn't before hand.

Gathering my resolve, I set out toward my proper course.

Usually, it was refreshing to come out here to the thicket in the evenings and listen to the nightingale sing and the crickets chirp, but tonight the woods were filled with terror.

It may have been my imagination, but I thought that I could hear it breathing, hot and heavy, down my neck behind me. I turned on my heels and fired twice in the direction I was certain the beast was in, only to find that I'd fired two of my rare bullets into the empty knot of a hollow tree that splintered open upon impact. No sooner had my ears finished ringing from the sound of the gunshot than I could feel the beast rushing behind me from the opposite direction. I was left no time to marvel at how fast he was, I simply had to turn as quickly as I could in hopes of catching it with a bullet.

But no sooner had I turned, the creature had vanished into the night air like so much vapor and mist.

Once more, I wiped the sweat from my brow with my lantern arm, the shadows were much more menacing in the changing light from all of the gnarled tree branches and dense foliage in the wooded area. As I had the lantern hanging high and my bicep absorbing my perspiration, that's when it hit me.

Square in the back, I was struck with all the force of his weight.

I could feel the pads of its feet and the clawed toes jam into my back, knocking me off balance. I lost my grip on both the lantern and the pistol and I could perceive them skittering off in front of me into the thick, matted grass of the forest floor. The lantern spilled open, leaking fire onto the ground, brightening the scene more and more as it burned up the dead branches. If I couldn't extricate myself soon, this whole region would be consumed in flame.

But first I had to deal with the beast.

I could feel the hot scratches deep into my skin as the creature dragged his paws and claws across my back. My shoulder grew hot; I could feel my blood spilling...

I knew if I was to survive, I had to do something drastic, but I was pinned. I tried hard to rotate to my right, to no avail, and then to my left, but the monster had me, dead to rights. I groaned under the strain and tried to leverage the wolf-man over me and that didn't work either.

His hairy digits we're reaching around my throat when I heard him squeal and whelp as though he'd been hurt, though clearly not at my hand, and then his grasp around my neck went limp. His weight no longer bore on me in its entirety, I was able to crawl a few feet away, putting me within arms reach of my pistol. Having no idea what was going on, I could tell that something had at least hurt the beast, because it was alternating between wailing in pain and snarling...

Finally, I was able to grab the gun and contort my body around, hoping to get a good shot, but the only thing staring back at me was my boy.

I coiled around to see the demon fleeing into the woods, the knife I left my boy with sticking out of its back, bleeding profusely all the while. My boy must have come out here, hoping to save me, and did.

He succeeded. But more than saving my life, he succeeded in making me forgetful of the torch burning down the forest.

We were left with only one course of action: to flee. Pursuit of the werewolf would have to wait.

Tonight, we would watch our old family home and surroundings burn to the ground under the light of the full moon and tomorrow the boy and I would begin our training. We would avenge our family and make sure the werewolf didn't live to see another night like this.

He was wounded and we'd be sure to discover his true identity in the morning light that was creeping up over the crackling fire. Oh yes, we would have our revenge.

A Simple Country Murder

Part One

Alvin Singer was fourteen years old, wheezed when he got excited, and wore a pair of horn-rimmed glasses that were still two sizes too big. The recent explosion of hormones in the boy had manifested itself in a number of ways, but most visibly with a smattering of acne across the landscape of his face. But the hormones had taken a much more insidious toll on the boy. For the last week, he'd had a completely inexplicable bulge in his pants. The phenomenon known as "an erection" was as foreign to the boy as a Siberian winter. The zipper of his jeans rubbing up against his crotch was the most titillating experience Alvin had ever experienced in his life. He'd heard stories about ways to deal with that problem, but each of them ended with trouble, and since he'd never been exposed to any sort of maturation program, any action he would take would be purely trial and error. He had theories about what would happen, but like any intelligent child with a quizzical mind, he simply had to experiment and test his hypotheses.

He chose a lovely spring day to test his theories out, when he would be at a large family gathering at his Aunt's house in the country. Her rural spread of land always served as the site of the annual Singer family picnic and the weather was always so beautiful and perfect that no one ever spent time in her expansive house. Deep in the bowels of her rural paradise was a rarely used bathroom and that is where Alvin decided he would try out his fleshy ideas. The night before the picnic he resolved to carry out his plan that next day and he spent hours in bed trying to sleep and resisting the urge to even think about his condition. But willpower is never as strong as biology and he spent his evening rubbing his entire midsection against a pillow, cuddling and caressing it, though he wasn't entirely sure why.

All of this was making him confused and crazy. Since no one talked about this at all, whether it was normal or disgusting or anything in between, he thought he was unique and broken.

Alvin woke up that morning feeling sheepish about his behaviour with the pillow the night before, not realizing that he no longer had the brain altering chemicals coursing through his body, forcing instinct and his proverbial second brain to take over completely. Nevertheless, he was steadfast in playing out the scientific methodology he'd chosen. In his mind, he was embarking on a great journey of discovery and in the name of science. He was as bold or daring as Louis Pasteur or Jonas Salk or Thomas Edison.

The drive out to the country with his parents was a tortuous forty-five minutes through the city and out into winding mountainous roads that burst through the rock into the lush and fertile river valley his relations had settled many, many years ago. He couldn't decide which was worse, the constant sniping between his mother and father, or the anticipation for his crime.

When they finally arrived, Alvin got out of the car, stretched his legs, and yawned. "Alvin," his mother shrieked, "make sure you've got enough bug spray."

She said that as though she was going to leave it up to him to apply, but she surprised him, squirting him on the back of the neck three times fast with a pumped spray of the repellant.

"Ow, mom," he said as he clutched his neck with his hand, which she quickly sprayed also. "Quit it!"

"Oh, hush up and put it on."

"Listen to your mother, son."

He rubbed the bug spray deep into his arms until they were dry.

Alvin and his parents walked around the front of the palatial estate on a soft soil path that led to the spacious, tree-lined private park behind it that over looked the mountain's river. The picturesque backyard contained no less than three gardens of flowers and as many more picnic tables, enough to seat most of the Singer clan. It was as idyllic as idyllic could be, but Alvin couldn't see the Shangri-La before him. All he could do was count the minutes until he could sneak away to the bathroom and vigorously scratch the itch boiling inside his confused, mid-pubescent body...or at least rub and massage it.

"Alvin," his Aunt yelled, excited to see him beyond all comprehension. Though she was at least a hundred pounds overweight and waddled everywhere she went, she seemed to teleport instantly in front of Alvin from across the yard to pinch his pimpled cheeks twice as hard as anyone should. So hard, in fact, that she didn't notice that she'd popped open one of his zits. It oozed puss onto her hand and if she did notice, she made no indication whatsoever. "How is my favorite nephew?"

"I'm good, Aunt Evelyn," Alvin squeaked.

"Oh my God, Joanie, he's growing up so fast, like a weed. And look at that big wide mouth, like a real teenager's. You're so grown up, Alvin."

"I'm working on it." But she didn't hear him. She waddled away with her sister, Alvin's mother, chattering like a school-yard gossip queen. Alvin's father retreated to a lawn chair overlooking the river with a few of the other Singer men to smoke cigars.

The younger children frolicked and laughed around the tire swing, playing tag and carrying on in a mood of general merriment. As the oldest of all of his cousins, Alvin had the option to join the children or keep to himself, but he wasn't at all sure how he should proceed in order to act as inconspicuously as possible. He wanted to fit in, but not attract too much attention. His conundrum forced him to stand there on the edge of the yard with his hands in his pockets. His indecision, without any rhyme or reason, stirred the fire in his loins and he knew at that moment that he could wait no longer.

"I need to go to the bathroom," he said out loud to no one in particular with a snap of his fingers. He pivoted on his heel and turned back toward the house, marching up to the sliding glass door at the back of the wide, redwood deck. That's where his Uncle Charlie, who spoke in a deep voice through his bristly, blonde moustache, promptly intercepted him. "Alvin, hello. How are you?"

"Good. Fine." Alvin tried rushing past him to no avail.

"Where's the fire, neph?"

"I have to go to the bathroom."

"Understood," Uncle Charlie chuckled and continued walking by, leaving Alvin to his intimate business.

There were no further obstacles en route to the guest bathroom, but Alvin was convinced he was pegged already for what he was about to do.

The bathroom was as expansive and ornate as the house itself. The walls inside were a light, creamy brown that offset the golden oak cabinets and shelves. The shelves were filled with cherubic knick-knacks in various poses. One enterprising young angel, wearing nothing but a quiver of arrows, was holding himself as though he himself had to use the restroom and was at the same time bashfully blowing a kiss to a plump female angel across the shelf.

Alvin carefully closed and locked the door behind him. The click of the lock echoed in the room.

An experiment with this much riding on it needed to be as free as possible from distractions or outside irritants that could influence the results, which is why Alvin began to strip. Nude was the only state of being appropriate for an experiment of this magnitude. He neatly folded each item of clothing as it came off and placed it fastidiously in a pile on the bookshelf next to the toilet. Once he was completely naked, Alvin sighed wistfully and wondered where to start. He took a few steps back and forth on the furry, black bath mat in front of the sink. The yarn felt good between his toes.

He decided the best course of action was to simply lay down on the floor and begin, which is exactly what he did.

Part Two

Alvin Singer stepped out onto the deck, closing the sliding door behind him. He felt nauseous, ready to throw up although his experiment had been a rousing success. He even enjoyed the process up until the time he was finished, and then he was more confused than anything. He took slow, careful steps toward the riverbank, thinking the whole time about his feelings. He couldn't decide if his desire to vomit came as a side effect of his experiment, or because of the overwhelming guilt he felt.

If ever he dared to try it again, he'd have to try to maintain his objectivity on the matter.

Thinking he might play with his cousins, Alvin went over to them, but when he got there, all he could think about was how they might think of him if they knew what he'd just done. He couldn't get that thought out of his head, no matter who at the party he looked at. How about Aunt Evelyn. Would she find it repulsive? And Uncle Charlie? Would he find it vile and disgusting? Alvin thought that if his mother knew or found out she might faint.

Soon, the guilt of what he'd done melted away and he found himself coming out of his morass and warming up to the other kids. They were still playing tag and one of them, a seven-year-old cousin of his named Cindy with stereotypical blonde hair and pigtails, rather boldly tagged him, "You're it!"

Instead of giving in to his urge to pout, he raced after her, almost completely forgetting the ordeal he'd just been through. "No tag backs! No tag backs!"

After thirty minutes or more of rigorous play he was back to normal, no longer obsessing over his experiment. He began to have a good time. So good a time, in fact, that he didn't notice Aunt Evelyn go into the house. She did catch his eye a few moments later when she reemerged in a panic. He couldn't hear her over the din of the river, but it was obvious she was calling Uncle Charlie over to her. As soon as he got near, she pulled him roughly down toward her so she could whisper excitedly into his ear. It didn't take her long to whip Uncle Charlie into a frenzy enough for action. Whatever the problem was, Uncle Charlie had to see it for himself, so he went through the sliding glass door. While he went in to investigate, Aunt Evelyn collapsed on the deck and wept. She was making such a big to do that it took no time at all for the rest of the adults to crowd around to comfort her. The commotion was so great even the children took notice, but before they could come any closer, Uncle Charlie came back out of the house with a dire look about him. He nodded to Alvin's father, Kevin, and Kevin met the children in the yard. "Children, children," he said to all of them with his hands raised in a paternal shushing motion, "I need you all to stay very calm. Something terrible has happened and I need you all to be on your best behaviour until the police arrive."

"What happened in there?" Alvin asked. Since he was the oldest of them, it only seemed natural.

Alvin's father cleared his throat and stated gravely, "There's been a murder."

Everyone was shocked, especially Alvin. He'd just been in the house and wondered to himself what would have happened if the murderer had crashed through the door, interrupting his experiment. It was too much for him to bear. He dwelled on it, feeling hollow inside until the police arrived.

Two cars came, one unmarked and one marked with flashing lights and a uniformed officer. The unmarked car brought a pair of detectives, dressed in shirts, ties, and fedoras. For every day of the rest of his life, Alvin would remember the image of the first detective out of the car, staring coldly through him and spitting the toothpick in his mouth out across five feet of grass.

The uniformed officer met with the detectives as soon as they all got out of their cars. They nodded and whispered at each other. They'd come up with their plan and went their separate ways. The detectives went toward the adults and the house and the uniformed officer came down to calm the children and keep them from contaminating the evidence. The officer took off his dark sunglasses and put on a smile. The gaggle of children was in awe of the policeman and began shouting a chorus of questions all at once at him.

He laughed, "One at a time, one at a time."

"What happened?" said Susan, Alvin's cousin by way of his mother's brother, Jerry. She was the youngest in her family.

"Well, there's been a pretty heinous crime committed inside, and right now the detectives are trying to get to the bottom of things."

"Uncle Kevin said there was a murder," little Billy Singer commented. He was Alvin's cousin by way of his mother's other sister, Suzanne.

"That's what the detectives are going to find out. If there was a murder, they'll figure out who did it and why."

It wasn't long before one of the detectives came outside with Uncle Charlie. They spoke for a moment and Alvin almost thought, just for a second, that Uncle Charlie gave him a look. But for the life of him, he couldn't figure out what kind of look it was. The detective sent Uncle Charlie back into the house and came back toward the flock of minors.

"Kids," said the officer, "This is Detective Lantz."

As though they were in school, most of the children parroted back, "Hello, Detective Lantz."

"Hello, kids. I need to talk to Alvin. Which one of you is Alvin?"

All the feelings of guilt and nausea returned to Alvin as he sheepishly raised his hand and cracked his voice to say, "I'm Alvin."

"Why don't you come with me, son."

"Oh," he coughed, "okay."

Detective Lantz led Alvin across the yard, in the house, across the living room and into the kitchen. "Alvin, this is my partner, Detective Walters, and we'd like to ask you a few questions. Why don't you take a seat?"

"Yes, sir."

Detective Walters had nothing to say, but sat and watched Alvin and Detective Lantz like a sharpshooter ready to fire. Alvin settled into his chair as Detective Lantz began, "Your...uncle? Right? Your Uncle Charlie said that you were the last person he saw enter house before the incident. Did you come into the house?"

"Yes, sir..."

"And what did you come into the house for?"

"I, uh... I had to go to the bathroom."

"And did you go straight to the bathroom, or did you make any stops along the way?"

"I went straight there, sir."

"Which bathroom did you use and which way did you take to get there?"

"Well, I guess I used the one downstairs, I came in through the back door and came through here and went downstairs."

"I see. And did you see anyone or anything suspicious on your way?"

"No, sir. Oh, wait. I did see Uncle Charlie on my way in."

"You saw your Uncle Charlie?"

"Yeah. We said hello and I came into the bathroom."

"Straight into the bathroom?"

"Yes, sir."

"And what did you do in the bathroom?"

"I...uh...I went to the bathroom, sir."

"Okay."

Alvin sat there, nodding quietly, until Detective Lantz asked another question after a measured pause. "And was there anyone outside the bathroom, waiting to go in?"

"Sir?"

"Outside the bathroom. After you were done. Was there anyone waiting to go in?"

"Not that I can recall, sir."

"So, as far as you know, you were the only one who used that bathroom from that time to this?"

"I guess so."

"I see," Lantz said, gravely.

His eyes shifted over to his partner, Walters. Walters took a deep, heavy breath. This was a man whose pervasive silence added gravitas to what little he did have to say. "We're obligated now to tell you that you're suspected of pre-conceptive murder in the first degree, Alvin. You have the right to remain silent. Anything you say can be used against you in a court of law. If you, or your parents, can't afford an attorney, one will be appointed to you."

Walters stood, withdrawing a pair of handcuffs off his belt from behind his suit jacket.

"Murder?" Alvin squeaked, "pre...what?"

Lantz raised a hand to Walters, delaying him for a moment. "Pre-conceptive murder. Ejaculation outside the womb. It's murder, Alvin. Didn't your parents ever tell you that? Didn't they ever tell you not to touch yourself?"

"Ummm..."

"This is a very grave crime. Every sperm deserves a chance at life and you tried flushing a million potential lives down the toilet.

Fortunately, that toilet is having problems and we caught you in the nick of time to make sure this never happens again."

"But..." Anxiety was rising in Alvin. Any guilt he thought he felt before was minor in comparison to the alarm sirens going off in his brain and consuming his chest with the nervous flickering of fiery dread. "But I didn't know..."

"You didn't know that murder was murder isn't an excuse that's going to work in the courts, Alvin. It's not an excuse for all the potential lives you ended. If you put a knife in somebody and they died, but you didn't know it was wrong doesn't make it any less so. And it doesn't make that person any less dead."

Meekly, not having any sort of answer or challenge to the authority of the detectives, Alvin quietly replied, "No, sir."

"And you killed a person that could have been."

A single, hot tear rolled down Alvin's cheek, and then another, and another, and then a dozen more. Shame leaked from his eyes as sure as each tear and each sob reinforced his sense of self-hatred for what he'd done.

Lantz nodded to Walters, chiding him to continue. Walters lifted Alvin up from the chair by the scruff of his collar, roughly binding his hands behind his back with the clanking metal cuffs. Walters whispered something in Alvin's ear that broke him. Alvin collapsed with this news, crying and sobbing, but Walters held him up by his underarm. "I'm sorry. I'm sorry. I'm so sorry. Please, please just let me go. I'm so, so sorry."

But sorry didn't cut it for a murder, even a pre-conceptive murder, and Detective Lantz said so.

"Please," Alvin whimpered. "No one told me... I'm so sorry. I'll never do it again. I'm so, so sorry."

They led Alvin out through the back door for all of his family to see. It was like a final kick in the gut for Alvin. He almost vomited when he registered the disgust in his mother's face. Only a few more tears had time to run down his face before his mother became so shamed and shocked that she fainted.

Alvin cried all the way to the squad car and for a long time after that. His whole way there he softly exclaimed his apologies between the hyperventilated breaths of an over-stimulated adolescent.

Walters stuffed Alvin into the car roughly and slammed the door shut behind him. Everyone could still hear Alvin crying behind the glass and metal of the car in all of his tortured agony.

Lantz and Walters stood next to the squad car, talking shop while they waited for the lab boys to arrive so they could fish the victims, the dead would-be American's, out of the toilet bowl for the evidence lock up.

"I hate to see it in kids this young. It doesn't feel right sometimes, locking 'em up, but I suppose it's better we get 'em off the streets now before they move up to post-conceptive murder."

"Yup," Walters croaked.

"It's astounding that in this day and age there are kids out there still who think they can get away with deviant behaviour like this."

"Yup," Walters croaked again.

"If it hadn't been for that leaky toilet this kid would'a got away with it. Then who knows how many potentials he'd have killed?"

"Yup," Walters croaked a third time.

As the forensics van pulled up behind the squad car, Lantz turned to his partner to ask a question that had been on his mind for the last few minutes, "So... What was it that you said to the kid?"

Walters squinted in thought for a moment, almost unconsciously watching the lab team step out of their van and march neatly toward the house. "I told him that the only person who hated him more than me for what he did was God."

"Too true," Lantz agreed. "Too true."

Bot Four

I want to go back to sleep. I don't know what that crash was, but it did wake me up. Shit. Fall back to sleep.

"The time is six-fifteen. Would you like to snooze for five minutes?"

Shit. The alarm clock.

"The time is six-fifteen and thirty-seconds. Would you like to snooze for five minutes?"

Fuck it. "No."

"Good morning, then." I'm up anyway, might as well get to work early. Maybe get some coffee. Forget the coffee, it makes me too excitable.

"Harold?"

"What dear?" Goddamn crash got her up too.

"Could you get some more milk and cheese on your way home today?" I hate going to the store. I hate buying milk and cheese.

"Of course, sweetheart. Why don't you go back to sleep?" She'll be out like a light soon. I better get in the shower.

Damn. The water's too cold and my work clothes are wrinkled. Just my luck. The robots at the Works will think I'm up to something. That's just what I need. "Fucking robots..."

"What was that, dear?" Shit. Did I say that out loud?

"Nothing, princess. Go back to sleep." I wish I could sleep in.

The ride to the Works takes too damn long, as usual. Damn conveyer roads. I'll be early for once, though. Maybe I'll give the foreman a bloody heart attack. It'd serve 'im right for what he did to Jonesy. Prick. Glad I'm not Jonesy though. Wouldn't trade him places in a million years.

"Works Building Four." About fucking time. Better not forget my briefcase. I could only imagine what sort of trouble I'd get in if I left my case on one of the public road cars. Oh. Here's my door.

"Hello, Engineer Liman." Fucking robots.

"Hello, Tad." Tad was short for CETAD. CETAD was an acronym for Cybernetic Employee Threat Analyzation Droid. Everyone calls him Tad. Everyone hates him.

"You are slightly earlier than usual. Working on a special project?" I wish they wouldn't subject us to Tad before letting us into the Works.

"No. Nothing like that, Tad." I chuckled. Why did I chuckle? He's going to think it's suspicious.

Fuck!

"Your static suit is wrinkled. Was your laundry unit malfunctioning last night, Engineer? Or were you working late?" Bad sign, he never believes the truth anyway.

"No..." He can feel the tension. He just has no idea where the hell it's coming from. "Nothing like that..."

That's his one fatal flaw. Everyone is nervous just talking to him because he's capable of hauling us away with no reason other than we might be "potential terrorist threats" to the Works based solely on his flawed perception.

"Would you like to talk about it?" He's probing. Fuck me, why is he probing?

"Uhhh... My wife forgot to put it in the laundry processor. Can I get to work, Tad?"

"What's the rush, Engineer?"

Fuck. He thinks I'm up to something.

"Just...eager to get to work."

"That isn't why you came early."

"There was a loud crash outside our bedroom this morning that woke me up a little early, is all. I'd appreciate it if you just let me get to work."

Fuck him.

"Very well, Engineer. But you are cleared Code Yellow Alert."

"As long as I can get to work." Code Yellow. That's exactly what I need. Fuck this guy. If he had a neck I'd wring it.

"You may pass, please report to room A-16 for your surveillance bot."

Shit. Code Yellow means he thinks I'm a potential threat so I'm under constant surveillance by a hover-cam surveillance bot. That's exactly what I need. My job isn't high pressure enough, I need a camera buzzing me all day.

"Hey Tyree." Tyree was the human monitor for the surveillance bots. He works in A-16.

"Harry! What brings you to Big Brother's front door?" He was a good fellow. Maybe he enjoyed his work a little too much, but I'm sure he's just glad to be alive after the accident in the gear core. Poor bastard got sent out to replace a cog and he came out missing an eye and three fingers. He got transferred here after that.

"Tad thinks I'm up to something."

"He does, does he?" Like I said, Tyree's a good guy. "What did you do to get his goat?"

"Not anything, really. I was a couple of minutes early and you know how jumpy he gets."

"That's the problem with a machine like that: his logic circuits only allow one interpretation of things. His logic circuits tell him he's good at picking up on people's vibes and he's really not." Amen. "Once in a while he's right, but not often. Knew a girl like that once. A real firecracker. Thought she could read anybody like a book, but she didn't know shit from shine-o-la. It was hard wired into her circuits, just like Taddy boy. It's faulty wiring. I just had to get rid of her."

"Why don't we get rid of Tad? Save a lot of problems that way."

"Can't. Old man won't have it. He trusts Tad to the grave. It's hardwired into his brain, too."

"Oh, well."

"Get used to it." I don't want to get used to it.

"I'll give you Bot-Four. He's a little twitchy, but he talks less than the others."

"I appreciate that." Lord, will I. The last thing I need is a chatty surveillance bot. "People shouldn't have to work in these conditions."

"You're right, but you know as well as I do that things won't change. It's the money that talks, not us."

"I suppose. Well, thanks again. I better get to work before Tad thinks I'm up to anything sinister."

"Don't sweat it."

Bot-Four asked me to calm down seven times between A-16 and station three-eight.

"Please...zzzt...calm down." Eight times.

"Please stop asking me to calm down."

"Until your blood pressure drops below danger levels, my pr...zzzt...gramming will not allow it." Great. How am I supposed to calm down with this goddamn hover-bot asking me to calm down every six seconds?

Just take a deep breath.

"Please...zzzt...calm down." Nine.

Nine fucking times.

Take a deep breath.

Take a deep breath and count to ten. That'll help.

One. Get to my workstation.

Two. I'll open my briefcase.

Three. Another deep breath. Fight the urge to kill it.

Four. Pull out my notes from yesterday.

Five. That's it. Get lost in your work.

Six. Focus, focus, focus.

"Please...zzzt...calm down."

He's dead. Fuck it.

All I can feel is how bad my knuckles hurt and how warm the blood running down my fingers is.

The tension in my chest goes away a little bit more with each savage blow to that little fucking asshole Bot-Four.

All I can hear is the sizzle of his circuits shorting.

I'm going to lose my job over this.

The Hero and the Horror

"Order! We will have order!" The town elder shouted over the din of his panicked townspeople. They had gathered at the town hall, an immense room with high echoing ceilings, thick beams, and a thatched roof. In better times, the town and its people would have been celebrating their idyllic lifestyle, in the way only a community of simple dairy farmers could. But now, a darkness had descended over them.

"One at a time, one at a time," he shouted again.

He pointed to one man, giving him permission to speak. "She's dead already. Let's just finish it."

A woman stood up, babe in arms, "But he said he'd kill us if we hurt her!"

"All of us!"

"But what do we do?"

"What can we do?"

"If we do nothing, this will go on forever and we'll live under his thumb."

"He'll kill us all, one way or the other."

"Cowards!" came one young voice. It was full of steel and resolve and did a better job silencing the crowd than the elder could do.

All eyes were on him. The elder narrowed his gaze and invited the boy to explain further. "And what should we do, young man?"

"We fight. We fight him and make a stand. We fight him while there is still enough of us left to resist him."

He dodged a piece of fruit thrown at him, "You're the coward! You only say such things because it's still the daytime and it's safe."

"When the sun goes down, none of us will be safe!"

The afflicted girl's mother sobbed loudly and the hall broke out into shouting once more. The village elder raised his hands, requesting stillness from the crowd. A hush fell over the townsfolk when they noticed their leader calling for quiet.

Slowly, he lowered his arms, timing the utterance from his lips for maximum dramatic impact, hoping that his words would resonate with his flock like a tuning fork. "We will hire a vampire hunter."

A few of the old maids gasped, but on the whole the audience sat in stunned silence. A few more in the back muttered things like, "We can't," and, "No," and, "It'll be the death of us all!" But they all knew that the elder's word was the law and a hunter would be hired from community funds and it would have to happen quickly. There were only two nights left before the girl's turn would be complete and the villain would be back to collect her. And now that an aggressive course of action had been decided on, every one lived on the edge of fear.

It was never wise to draw the ire of a vampire, and the townsfolk didn't know if there were any familiars among their number loyal to their sworn enemy, and they didn't know if they'd even be able to find a hunter, let alone one knowledgeable enough to vanquish an immortal.

The town spent the next night unable to sleep for fear of attack. They were still uneasy from the last assault waged against them. The moon was full and the night was crisp and cool with the approaching autumn. It began as a low howling and a foul smell on the wind, and the howl turned into a shrill shriek through leafless tree branches. On the wind came the sound of leather wings flapping toward them in the night.

The girl had been at the artesian well fetching water for her mother when the breeze turned foul. The vampire ran her down on the cobblestone of the town's single road. He ravaged and infected her, then deposited her at home, leaving his warning with her parents. Since then, a tangible fear had grown in the air of the town. It doubled itself with their commitment to fight. If you focused hard enough, you could almost taste it. It was coppery, like blood, almost enough to make one heave.

The boy who insisted they fight was given the task of finding a man suitable for the job and rode out of town immediately in search of a champion. Half of the town thought he'd been sent on a fool's errand, the other half thought he'd been sent to save them all.

Perhaps both were true.

Night fell once more on the village, and it was the night the girl would be turned fully, and ready for the vampire's inevitable and momentous return. When the sun fell, the low wind returned, and one by one, each and every door was barricaded shut and every window shuttered. Crosses were worn around as many necks as they had crucifixes.

It was anyone's guess if they would find the salvation they asked for in the prayers they all made.

Over the soft howling of the wind came the evenly paced clippity-clop of a shoed horse alongside the slow shuffling footstep of a tired man who had walked a long way.

Curious eyes peered through shutters and curtains, hoping to catch a glimpse of the arriving stranger. They recognized the boy leading the horse right off. He must have accomplished his mission, because atop his horse rode a man. He was dressed in all manner of straps and buckles with a striking red scarf that fluttered behind him.

The instinct was to run out and greet the man who could be their saviour, but the uncertainty of their tormentor's time of arrival kept them all indoors. The fear was understandable to the stranger. He felt that way once, too. Long ago. He didn't hold their ingratitude against them.

The boy led him straight to the village elder's house so that he might palaver with their leader. Tea and biscuits were laid out, but the stranger paid them no mind. He seemed to ask for the situation without speaking. He meant business and you could tell from the resolve in his eyes and the slow, deliberate nature of his movement and posture. He was like a great stonewall, which was somehow comforting and unsettling all at once.

"A fortnight ago it first appeared. It killed a boy, herding goats in the pastures. Even though he was drained of blood, we thought for a while it was a wolf. We assembled our brute squad and hounds, looking for it high and low, but we found no trace. That's when we noticed the lights on the mountain. We approached, but something attacked us. We lost two men there. Then three nights ago, he came for the girl, to turn her.

"He left her with her parents, we don't know why. He said he'd be back for her three days hence, tonight."

The stranger broke his silence in a deep voice that commanded respect, but had a soft empathy to it that could only come from pain. "He left her here to feed. From his fortress, he'll not be able to feed her enough when the thirst hits her."

"My god. She could kill us all."

"Mayhap. Take me to her."

They took him to the girl's house by torchlight. The village elder beat heavily three times upon the door. The girl's father, the cobbler, unbolted and opened it, wary of the stranger and the looming threat in the dark beyond. His somber countenance kept him from speaking as he led the three men to the slumbering corpse that was once his daughter.

He opened the thick oaken door that led to her room. Her mother hunched over her, crying. The flickering gaslight gave the small room all the appearance of a haunted house, casting long, distorted shadows that moved in unnatural ways across the dark wood walls.

The stranger put a firm but gentle hand on the mother's shoulder and spoke calmly. "You should go."

"I'm not leaving my little girl."

"You don't want to see what happens next."

"She's my baby," she sobbed, "I'm not going anywhere."

"Suit yourself."

The stranger startled everyone with the speed of his reaction. In the space of a breath, he'd drawn a wooden dagger and plunged it deep and true into the young girl's heart.

Thick, mostly congealed blood splashed across them all upon the force of impact. What was left oozed out of the gaping wound.

The girl was making a gurgling noise that was something like an angry cat under water. That unsettling sound was barely audible over the wailing screams of the mother. With great effort, the mother stood and beat her fists on the side of the stranger with all the effect of a wooden arrow shot into a stone block.

It was at that moment a concussive force blew through the room, shattering the windows into tiny particles, blasting the shutters off their hinges, and tearing the curtains down, blowing them across the room. Everyone was knocked to the ground, save the stranger, who looked up, out the window, slowly and defiantly. The sound of beating leather wings grew louder and louder until the vampire himself descended through the window. He raised his hand, ending the torrent of wind and glass.

Silence.

A deep, unnatural silence.

The vampire, pale in complexion, dark in the eyes, and long in the tooth, stood over the now completely dead girl.

The stranger made no move or sound, giving the beast ample time to inspect his handiwork. The vampire sniffed once sharply in the air and fingered the pinewood stake with a gnarled claw.

Finally, filled with pain, he broke the silence. "She was to have been my Queen."

The stranger said nothing.

"I was quite clear with her parents what the consequences were for such insolence."

Again, the stranger said nothing. The vampire looked up with his black eyes. They sparkled in the gaslight, giving the monster an unnatural charisma that felt unnerving. Nothing that lethal should seem so reasonable, calm, and hurt.

It was frightening to everyone.

Everyone save the stranger.

In his arrogance, the vampire turned from the stranger and their audience and looked down sadly to regard the girl. "Such a pity. You could have all been my slaves, the entire village. Instead, you'll all have to die."

"Think again."

To all in the room, it seemed merely like the vampire had grabbed his face in agony, apropos of nothing. The stranger had made his move and no one had even noticed, least of all the vampire, too busy coddling his own hubris. It was a vial of holy water and garlic cloves that smashed into the face of the vampire at incredible velocity and had all the effect of an acid. The vampire let out a deep roar of pain and revealed his true form.

Long claws grew from his fingers and great leathery wings stretched and pulled through the fabric of his cloak. His face, disfigured from the acid, transformed into something terrifying. His brow swelled into an angry furrow, his eyes turned the yellow of rotten egg yolk, his nose and teeth sharpened, and his skin took on all the pallor of the undead. Sores and dripping pustules of mucous and liquid molted from his face, leftover from the sneak attack of the stranger.

He howled a sick scream that reverberated in the very souls of those watching. Then he lunged for the stranger.

The stranger sidestepped and planted an elbow into the side of the vampires head, but it did little to deter his attack. The vampire planted his palm into the stranger's chest, knocking the wind from him and sending him reeling against the back wall.

It was the first time the townsfolk had seen him falter. If their hearts hadn't been filled with so much fright from the true form of the vampire, they'd be filled with despair. If the stranger lost, the ramifications for their little village would be enormous. They would all die in agony, torn apart limb from limb, their blood used as fuel and fodder for their tormenter. It was not a happy prospect.

The stranger stood, turning the situation to his advantage, smashing another vial of holy water into the vampire's face, obscuring his vision. With one graceful movement, he got his footing back and swung his fist hard into the vampire's left temple.

"Arrogant knave! You think you can stand against an immortal?"

Ignoring the taunts, the stranger flicked garlic soaked, wooden shards at the beast to no effect.

"I've stood against better."

The stranger charged. He and the beast met in the center of the room, over the corpse of the girl.

They were locked together. None of the spectators knew who would come out on top. With the cloaks and folded wings, no one could see the damage they'd done to each other. Had the stranger vanquished their unholy bane? Or had the vampire come out on top, ending the life of their would-be protector?

It was the gurgling sound of congealed blood dripping down to the floor that tipped them off that the monster might have been bested.

The vampire held the face of the stranger tightly, digging his claws into his face, drawing blood. "It's not over for you."

With great strain, fighting it every step of the way, life escaped the vampire. Slowly, the stranger lowered the miscreation to the floor so they could all see the wooden blade buried deeply in the monster's heart.

A collective sigh of relief could be felt throughout the spectators in the room. "You've done it," the boy exclaimed.

"Aye."

It was then that he faltered to his knees.

"What's wrong?" The boy leapt to the stranger's side. "What did he mean it wasn't over?"

The stranger revealed a deep gash across his neck, already infected with a necrotic blackness. "It is finished."

And he collapsed into the boy's arms.

The dead girl's mother found her way into her husband's arms. The village elder placed his hands on the boy's shoulder, deeply wounded by the loss of their hero. If it hadn't been for all the bloodshed and loss, the scene might have been an idyllic painting in a museum.

At first light, the villagers burned, in a massive pyre, the corpses of the vampire and his hunter. After the fires died, the townsfolk went back to their lives, trying as hard as they could to forget this episode in their town's history.

But one in their number couldn't forget.

Forged over the coals and embers of the funeral pyre of their hero and tormentor was the resolve of the boy. Then and there he made a solemn vow to carry on the work of a vampire hunter. Never would a village or town fall prey to the fancies of the unholy undead where he could help it.

The village didn't understand his desire to fight in the first place, they certainly would not understand his desire to fight now. And so he left the village without a single goodbye.

His work was just beginning.

The Train from Hell to Heaven

I have been dead for a very long time. I wouldn't know how long a time. In Hell time doesn't work as it used to up there on the surface. But whatever time we do have down here, we pass it by doing this and that. Those of us that are down here used to be very bad people. We have been cured of that. We have come to understand the error of our ways. We have been looked down upon as we used to look down upon others and we came to realize it was not a very pleasant.

Most of us have been cured, anyway. There are a few rare exceptions. Occasionally I play Whist with a few of the guys: Julius Caesar and Presidents Nixon and Reagan. I never knew of Reagan or Nixon on Earth, they were well after my time. Nixon was as vicious now as I have been told he was during his time up there. He still hates people, which I don't understand.

I used to hate people too, but I don't hate anyone anymore.

Before we get too far along, I ought to mention who I am. I may seem a bit off-putting to people. I was quite a notorious monster in my life upstairs and after an eternity thinking about what I had done, I have become quite ashamed of myself. Please do not judge me by who I was. Much as it pains me to tell you, the sad fact of the matter is that my name is Hitler and I ordered the deaths of many people and I ordered the out and out hatred of as many more.

I used to be proud of what I had done, but I am no longer.

I had read once, posthumously, of course, a story in which I had asked to have a statue erected of me in New York in front of the United Nations building with a plaque reading, "I beg your pardon."

I would very much like a plaque bearing that message, but not the statue. I would rather the world forgot my image. That isn't to say that I wouldn't like the world to learn from my atrocities (read: mistakes). I would very much like the world to realize that killing their fellow humans, regardless of our differences, is never a good idea. Being in Hell, you get a broad sense of what's going on up there, we get the daily papers and magazines and the like, and it rather surprises me that I didn't do a better job of turning people off of war forever.

I certainly made a go of it.

Anyhow, I was going to tell you what I have decided to do. I have decided to find my way up to Heaven, or at least the pearly gates Saint Peter guards, and apologize to as many of my victims as I can find. I will be gracious, I will hold my hat in my hands, and I will hang my head low in shame. We Germans do have pride, and I will show them what it is to see a proud German apologize.

What an apology it will be!

I had thought over the possibility of wearing my old uniform. It had always offered me an overwhelming sense of dignity, but I realized I did not deserve dignity. The swastika that I had so proudly worn should never be worn as a mark of pride again. Oh, how I had ruined it! Then I thought it might be an excellent gesture to go in my uniform but with all the badges and decorations torn off, but I decided finally to wear merely a set of old clothes and a woolen scarf. I would look as though I was tramp roaming the railroads of America. And, as the ultimate sign of respect, I would wear a Star of David on my chest with pride.

I deserve nothing less.

I've imagined it a hundred thousand times or more. I'd humble myself; I'd lower my shoulders and present myself meekly.

Saint Peter would ask me, "And what was your name?"

And I would say, "Adolf..."

And he would reply to me, in the delicate tones of angels, "I'm dreadfully sorry Adolf, but you've got the wrong gates."

"I know." That is where I would take my hat off. I'd hold it in my hands and hang my head some more. "I was wondering if it was possible if I could..."

"Could what? Out with it."

"Would it be possible, for me to, perhaps, apologize to those I've wronged? I know I'm not welcome here, but it would mean a lot to me if I could at least apologize."

I imagine Saint Peter would stroke his beard and contemplate the question. After a while he would give a stern "Hrmmmm..." Then, "It's a bit against the rules, I'm afraid, but if you wait here, I'll go in and see if anyone wants to come to the gate and let you speak to them."

I imagine a hundred thousand might come, perhaps as many as a million. Most, I believe, will want to throw fruit at me and yell and shout at me. A few, I expect, might be gracious enough to accept my humble apologies.

It matters little to me how they react. Those that yell might feel some satisfaction in shouting me down and those that don't might find some further peace in their afterlives.

While playing Whist, I spoke of my plans. Nixon was shocked, "Why would you want to go up there and make an ass of yourself by going and doing a thing like that?"

"I think it will do a lot of people good."

"Why do them any good? They're the reason you're here."

"Dick, don't you understand? I'm the reason I'm here. Perhaps some benefit to them might be found in my bringing myself before them. Perhaps it will relieve the feelings of guilt I have."

"Guilt? What's to feel guilty for? I'd never apologize for the people I hurt. They're just collateral damage."

Nixon couldn't wrap his head around it.

Reagan had an easier time, but still had a problem with the apology part of the plan. "You know, I did a lot of things I'm not proud of, and maybe I'm sorry for them, but why would I go out of my way to apologize? I did what I thought I had to and I let my own guilt suffer for it. I thought about going up there once or twice, you know, to apologize to a few of the soldiers who died at the hands of Iranians with weapons I sold them, but what good would it do? They're still dead, nothing I could say would bring them back or right the wrong I did."

After a moment of speaking, Reagan began muttering about what his wife, Nancy, would have told him to do. All of his conversations invariably ended with the same statement: "God, I miss her..."

Julius, I think, had the best advice, "Brutus apologized to me after a time. After a while to truly reflect, I think, perhaps, it was I who owed he the apology, but people do what they think is best for themselves and their countries, and few people stop to think about those they affect until they arrive here. An apology might not bring those you've wronged back from the eternal, but it would certainly make them understand that they weigh heavily upon your mind. It's some satisfaction, and in the eternal world we now reside, what else have we?"

I nodded my head pensively, as though I was weighing all of their advice. I did not want them all to know I thought old Julius was right.

Not yet, anyway.

I went home after our gentleman's game was over. Sadly, I had no one to go home to. Eva had left me when we got here. She couldn't forgive me for how wrong I had been. Before we died in each other's arms, I had told her that we would be together in Heaven and yet here we were.

Boy, was I wrong!

I had dallied with women here and there since my time in Hell began: Joan Rivers, Cleopatra, Susan B. Anthony, and others. There were more that you wouldn't know like Grace Anderson. She used to beat her children and kill kittens, but became as gentle as one when she came here. She was a delicate lover but after a while, in eternity, people get boring and we drift our separate ways. It happens everywhere all the time. The story is always the same although the details differ, but I will not bore you with them here.

Packing for my trip was easy. What could I pack?

I stitched a Star of David on my beggar's clothes and put them on. I wrapped my tattered scarf around my neck and was on my way.

Saint Peter and the Pearly Gates, here I come!

My journey began with ease. I simply strolled on my way out of town. I stopped at a shop now and again to say farewell to a few people that had become central to my life. The girl who sold me my morning coffee told me she would miss me. The young boy who delivered my morning newspapers gave me a Time magazine to read on the train. He was a sad case, full of sorrow. He had raped and killed a young girl his age, I would guess around thirteen years old. Her father killed the newspaper boy. Now he could barely stand the grief over what he had done.

As I passed by a whorehouse, a beautiful young girl came out to the sidewalk, "Fancy a fuck, mister?"

It seemed as though all the girls in Hell were young and beautiful. It was no difficult thing to do. You could be any age you wished as long as you lived it on Earth. I myself was a respectable 35 years old. I was 20 for a time, but being a young artist didn't suit me for very long. At 35 I was full of ambition and fire in my belly, wanting to make things better. "Not now, my dear. I have things to do."

Again, I was almost sidetracked by the heavenly smell of schnitzel. One doesn't have to eat in Hell since it is impossible to die, but there are times when your soul needs to eat food because it misses the feeling. But I was certainly on a mission. I could worry about the schnitzel later.

The train that linked Heaven and Hell was quite a walk, but I had all the time in the world. I never quite understood why they had the train, but you were free to head to the other side as often as you like. I suppose there were visitors from Heaven who came down to see lost loved ones now and again, but I had never fancied going up there myself before.

My seat was in the back of a crowded passenger car. I took it and found myself in the middle of a family. There was a mother and her three daughters dressed in their best Sunday clothes. Sitting directly across from me was the smallest of the girls. Her hair was pulled into two adorable pigtails and her face was pink with newness and love. She was perhaps five or six years old.

She smiled at me and I smiled back.

She waved at me and I waved back.

"Hello," she squeaked in her wonderful child voice. "My name is Susan."

"Hello, Susan."

"What's your name?"

"People call me Adolf."

"Hello, Mister Adolf."

"How old are you, Susan?"

She held up all five plump fingers on her right hand.

"Susan!" Her mother shouted at us, interrupting the tender moment. "How many times have I told you not to speak to strangers?"

"I'm sorry ma'am. It was my fault entirely."

She gasped when she realized who I was. I'm told my mustache is quite recognizable and uniquely mine. After I explained to Susan's mother what I was doing, she warmed up to me considerably. She said that more people should think about doing what I was attempting.

By the time we got to the gates, she had explained to me why she was visiting Hell in the first place. You see, her husband had killed the whole family with a shotgun and then took his own life. It was quite terrible. Although their father had robbed them of their one chance at mortality, they still loved him unconditionally. Every so often, they would beg their mother to take them on the train to visit their father. He hated seeing them because they were a constant reminder of the wrong he had done, but he loved being with them.

A conductor yelled, "Next stop, Saint Peter's Gates!"

I shook hands with Susan's mother and said goodbye to Susan, touching her lightly on the nose. They filed into the gates with everyone else.

Susan had forced me to show fondness and that hurt me a little. I was determined to be meek and she had forced me to betray that. I hunched my shoulders and, with a sigh, further furrowed my posture. I wanted to look like the broken man I felt myself to be.

Soon, everyone had flooded into the gates and only Saint Peter was left. He and I were alone on the cloudy platform.

Saint Peter pushed his glasses back to the top of his nose and looked down at me from his Holy book, behind his immense, white podium.

I took my hat off and held it in both hands. I couldn't bring words to my mouth. A weight fell on my chest. I didn't expect to be brought speechless by the sight of Heaven's gate.

Saint Peter shook his head expectantly and gave me a once over. "Oh. It's you."

"Me, sir?" I had found my voice, but it was that of a field mouse.

"I was wondering when you were going to show up."

"I was..." I couldn't help but stutter. "I was hoping, perhaps... I might be..." I hadn't noticed that I was wringing my hat in my hands.

I was nervous!

I was one of the worlds greatest orators and here I was twitching nervously and stuttering. I was able to have stadiums of people hanging upon my every word and by the end of my speech they would go out and murder people on my behalf and now I could not form a sentence. "Might I be permitted... just for a moment.... To... uh.... I would like to apologize to those I've wronged."

"Of course you can."

"I can?"

"My dear Adolf, you have always been welcome through these gates. You have come here seeking forgiveness and what you may not have realized is that God *is* forgiveness. You may enter here and dwell in Heaven and apologize personally to everyone affected by your tirade on Earth."

My heart soared.

"Some might still feel slighted or somehow cheated, others will forgive you, but all of them will be respectful and listen to you."

I didn't feel as though I deserved treatment as good as this. I said so.

"Of course you do. You are a son of Adam. You are God's creation. Do you remember nothing that Jesus spoke of? Of course, you are welcome here and you certainly deserve this. All of God's people deserve this and more. That is what people fail to realize during their time on Earth. There could be a Heaven on Earth if people realized that they all deserve to be given the best."

"This..."

Saint Peter cut me off, "Say no more, Adolf. Go inside."

The gates opened. For me. They opened for me. The gates of Heaven allowed Adolf Hitler entrance.

I put my hat on and started in, toward the bright light. Saint Peter said one more thing to me as I passed him, "Get going, you've got a lot of work to do."

He was right.

Late Term Abortion

"Honey, I want to have an abortion."

"Again?" Harold asked his wife, Gladys. He'd been dodging her on the subject all week.

"I just can't bear it anymore. It's going to be more trouble if we wait any longer." She had her heart set on abortion. What could he do?

"Can we talk about this later?" Harold turned the page of his newspaper, hoping to emphasize that he was too busy relaxing to bother with such weighty talk.

"I just want it over with. It's hard enough, I'd rather do it while my mind is set."

Not looking up from his sports section, "Now, Dear. Let's not be hasty."

"I'm not being hasty. I've been thinking about it for months. We both have. You just don't have the nerve to say so."

Maybe she was right, he thought. Then, resigning himself, "Maybe you're right."

"Of course I'm right."

She seemed satisfied.

Harold sternly added, "You'll have to tell him, though. I had to tell his brother. You can tell him."

"Fine. I'll make the appointment and then we'll go up and tell him together." Gladys left the room to get on the phone, to ready her late term abortion.

"Yes. My name is Gladys Harper. I'd like to schedule an abortion..." All Harold could hear from the other end was a low toned buzz humming on and off in a secretarial cadence. "Yes. His name is Jeremy Harper. He's sixteen years old."

Harold shook his head, still trying to read his paper; trying hard not to pay attention to the phone conversation. "Well, he's just not turning out the way he's supposed to. I mean, he even applied to an art school not long ago. It's just shameful. Can you believe it?"

Harold couldn't believe it. And the only reason he agreed to the abortion was his overriding morality. He'd be damned to have a child of his turn into some type of Godforsaken hippy. He'd hoped that the boy would simply straighten out, but Jeremy had only gotten worse in the last three months.

The House and Senate passed the Late Term Abortion Act into law just before Jeremy's older brother, Bobby, was born. Gladys and Harold's commitment to abort Bobby stemmed from his decision to join the Communist Party in high school. They thought the idea of sharing something as sacred as money with less fortunate people was nothing short of dangerous and against God.

So they had him aborted.

Almost everyone thought it was easier to abort someone with bad ideas than to listen to them, but you could only abort your own children and you only had until their eighteenth birthday to organize it. After that, you were on your own. You had to let anyone who had grown full term say whatever they wanted to. Some clever children faked being obedient and made it full term. Afterwards, they elected to say things like, "The President is a mother fucker." Or, "Late term abortions are evil." Or, "We should give a fair share of money to the poor." They could say things like this whenever they wanted to.

More often than not, they were simply run out of town at that point.

Nowadays, people seemed happier agreeing with each other and running those that disagreed out of town. It was easier when they were younger though. They could simply schedule an appointment and wipe out their "childish mistakes."

"All right then, we'll be there Tuesday the eighth. Thank you very much... Uh-huh... You, too. Buh-bye." Gladys hung up the phone and took a deep breath. "All right Harold. The appointment is set for next Tuesday. Let's go tell him."

"You're sure you're not going to change your mind? We still have a couple of years..."

"No. The appointment is made and my mind is set." Then, as an afterthought, "Besides, we'll be able to take that trip to Hawaii this year instead of the year after next."

"Fine, but like I said, you're telling him."

They went upstairs together, holding each other by the arm for strength and moral support.

The door to his room was shut. Tacked clumsily to it was an upside down "Y" with a line intersecting it down the center encompassed by a circle. Gladys shuddered at the sight of it. The symbol was recognized widely as meaning this: peace.

Gently, Harold knocked on the door.

His voiced muffled through the wood, Jeremy called out, "Come in if you want."

Harold swung the door wide, allowing his wife to go in first. The posters of Che Guevara and Marilyn Monroe forced a hard gasp from her chest. So disgusted by this display, she couldn't make eye contact with her son, her monster.

His father tried making eye contact with him, but quickly looked down at his feet as soon as he did, ashamed of himself.

Not for the decision he and his wife just made, but because his son had turned into some type of devil monster.

Jeremy was sitting on his bed, reading a book. He set it down, meeting his parents' silence head on, calmly combating it with this, "You've come to abort me. Haven't you?"

Silence.

Harold was resigned to say nothing.

Gladys was trying hard to form words, but none came. Harold touched her back, indicating that it was her turn to speak. This worked. "Yes! We're here to abort you, you ungrateful little bastard!"

She screamed this, hoping it would force similar emotions from Jeremy, hoping that he would show some remorse for the evil he'd been doing.

"Okay." Jeremy said this as calmly as he'd ever said anything in his life.

Gladys moaned, wounded further, "How can you treat us like this? Can't you feel guilt?"

The boy thought about this for a moment, then coolly: "Certainly. When I've done something wrong."

This was too much for Harold, "Don't you talk back to your mother like that. Can't you see the damage you've already done to her?"

"It's all in her head." Jeremy was quick-tongued now that he had nothing left to lose.

"All in her head? You're a terror! Sent by the devil!"

"Why is that?"

Jeremy truly didn't know.

Gladys continued her sobbing and moaning. Harold pulled her under a consoling arm, growing ever more outraged with his only remaining son, "Why is that? How could you dare ask me such a thing!"

"Why am I evil for asking why?"

"Because you don't know better!"

"Maybe you don't know better."

"You've made me ashamed that I tried to defend you from this abortion. Your liberal politics, your constant questioning of authority and this art school nonsense has gone too far."

"Okay."

Gladys broke down on the floor, sobbing uncontrollably. Tears began to well in Harold's eyes, as well.

"Don't cry. It's all right. I don't want to live anyway if I can't do or say as I please."

"There's a special place in hell reserved for people like you..." Harold was so mad he didn't know if he should shit or go blind.

Then, screeching from the floor, Gladys wished her son well, "I hope you rot in hell for ever and all eternity, you little monster!"

"Me too. So long as I'm allowed to say so."

Jeremy wanted to end this episode by insulting and offending his parents as much as possible, he wanted them to sob and wail like babies.

He wanted to hurt them in a way they couldn't imagine. This is what he said to hurt them: "If God is okay with this, then he's a mother-fucker."

It worked.

Their wails and sobs filled Jeremy with enough peace to take him to his grave, where he'd be laid down to rest Tuesday, which was as fast as his mother could arrange it.

A Peculiar Constitutional

My wife and I often take a constitutional most evenings after I arrive home from work with our feline companion, Chester. This particular evening in question, I was intrigued by an invitation my wife received from our mutual friend, Miss Harriet P. Stander. Miss Stander had requested our presence this evening for a rendezvous on her front porch for beverages in order that we might behold a marvel in her possession that she assured us simply couldn't be described in words.

The sojourn to Miss Stander's house was perhaps a mile on foot and as Chester, my wife, and I walked, we had a lovely conversation abut assorted things of various natures.

My wife marveled at the weather and the sorts of flowers in bloom. I myself pondered aloud about the status of politics and the upcoming election. Chester, meanwhile, offered us a fascinating epiphany he'd had regarding the meaninglessness of life and the ever-expanding nature of the universe and cosmos. It was all a bit over my head, but the sciences had never been my strongest suit.

Chester was a devilishly intelligent cat that often confounded me with the depth of his learned philosophy.

It was no wonder I enjoyed his company.

My wife enjoyed him for altogether different reasons. She was barren, you see, and Chester tolerated quite admirably her predilection to groom and pamper a child-sized creature of intelligence. It was her life's goal, it seemed, to always make sure that at all times Chester had tied, snugly around his neck, an ornately ribboned bow-tie.

Were I a jealous man, I might be upset about the time spent gossiping between the pair while my wife manicured his hands and pedicured his feet. But he was a cat and such notions were absolute poppycock. He was a handsome cat, to be sure, but still just a cat.

We arrived promptly at Miss Stander's to find that she'd been waiting for us on her porch with mint juleps and iced tea.

"Mister Book, Missus Book." She greeted us politely, but considered Chester and a look of consternation arrived on her face like a train pulling into a station. "Chester," she added with coldness.

Chester and I both tipped our hats politely at Miss Stander and my wife offered a doubly polite curtsy.

"Mister Book, might you and your feline companion care to sit while I have a private word inside with Missus Book for a moment?"

I nodded to Chester and he bowed low, answering for us both, "We'd be most delighted, Ma'am."

"Wonderful."

She and Missus Book awayed through the front door. Chester began to speak as soon as he was confident they were out of earshot. "I'm not quite sure she likes me, James."

"Pish posh. I wouldn't say that, Chester. She's had us all over before."

"True, to be sure, but something in her demeanor was indeed disconcerting."

"In all truth, she did seem at least modestly discombobulated by your presence."

"Discombobulated indeed."

"Perhaps she has a guest over with an allergy to cats?"

"Hardly likely."

It was then that my wife and Miss Stander came from within her lovely abode. Chester and I stood up quickly and remained standing until they took their seats on the porch to either side of us.

"I do hope everything is all correct, Ma'am."

"All correct, indeed, Mister Cat. I have spoken things over with Missus Book and she has promised me that you will be on your best behaviour."

"You wound me, Madame. Have you known my behaviour to ever be less than best?"

"No, Mister Cat, which is why I've agreed to let you stay for this exhibition."

"I appreciate your honesty, Ma'am. I assure you that my behaviour will never have been better."

"Would you all like a drink before we begin?"

We all agreed that beverages would be delightful and she passed around cold, sweating cups. Chester and I opted for the mint juleps while the ladies opted for the iced tea, though Miss Stander assured my wife that there was a healthy dose of bourbon in the tea.

The four of us sat there, fanning ourselves in the heat, sipping our libations and discussing nothing in particular until Missus Book politely asked what it was the invitation to come over was all about.

"Well," Miss Stander answered, "the oddity I've come across is so amazing I just had to show it to you. Merely telling you about it would not do it one bit of justice. And it's so adorable it just makes my heart melt."

"You've certainly piqued my curiosity, and I'm sure Missus Book's as well."

"Mine is aroused to no end," Chester added.

"Of that, I have no doubt, Mister Cat."

"Well, what is it, then, Miss Stander?"

"Best just to show you."

Miss Stander rose from her chair and went inside her house to retrieve her unspeakable curiosity while the three of us remained outside, sipping our drinks. I could tell by the crooked smile on my wife's face that she had at the very least some inkling about what we were about to behold.

Chester licked his lips and speculated, "I'm wondering if it has anything to do with a natural enemy of the *Felis Catus*."

"And why would that be, Chester?"

Chester put his drink down on the table and rested his furry paws on his rounded belly. "Well, James, why else would my presence, which is normally welcomed with open arms, be met with such incredulous apprehension?"

"And you think some manner of fish or bird or rat might be the object of her mystery?"

"What else could it be?"

"But there's nothing inherently spectacular or marvelous about any of those things. Perhaps it's something else. Those are much too mundane to be wondrous."

"Maybe a new style of *Nepeta cataria* she's cultivated?"

"Anything is more logical than a simple animal."

"We'll see, James. We'll see."

"Oh, would you two stop arguing? Whatever it is, no matter how mundane or stupendous, we'll all smile and nod and treat it with a healthy and polite sense of awe as befits Miss Stander's hospitality."

"Yes, love."

"I can agree to that, Lilly."

It was another moment or two before Miss Stander appeared back on the porch, her hands cupped around the item of our intense mental acquisitiveness.

"It's certainly smaller than a bread box..."

She sat down in her chair and placed the oddity on the table.

It was indeed truly wondrous and words fail me. Chester was right to a degree in his initial conjecture of a natural enemy of a feline. The small animal running about on the tabletop was indeed mouse-like, but it was a natural aberration, a mutated variant on a standard mouse that made it bizarre and worthy of a circus sideshow, but was at the same time alluring and awe-inspiring.

The mouse, if you could call it that, had soft white fur all around and a pink tail. Clearly it was albino, but that wasn't the most astounding thing about it. It had three legs but two heads and two sets of pink little eyes. Its hind legs were proper, but its heads were propped up by a lone leg centered beneath them. As it scurried around the table, every other step would cause it to pop up as though it were an acrobat.

It was indeed a sight to behold. The mouse was adorable, unique, and an amazing bit of nature brought to the civilization of Miss Stander's home. Our proverbial jaws dropped.

Except for Chester.

I had to admire the cat. His claws were dug into the side of the chair as though he was being propelled by automobile at great speed. His mouth was wired shut and he was perfectly still save for the even breathing in his chest and his eyes darting back and forth, following each and every movement of the two-headed mouse like a predator.

It was no wonder Miss Stander was wary of Chester's presence. This twilight visitation would sap him of any and all willpower for weeks to come. Self-restraint was a difficult skill to master, and as intelligent and well mannered as Chester was, he was still very much a slave to his own instinct.

"You all right Chester?"

Through clenched teeth he made a sound in the affirmative.

I was very proud of him.

"Isn't this just the cutest, most amazing little thing you've ever seen?"

"Very much, so," my wife replied.

"Where did you find him?" I asked

"Well, I was out in town and was doing some shopping for trinkets and knickknacks as I often do on my Saturday afternoons, you know, just to get out of the house and there was a Chinese street vendor in front of my favorite store selling odds and ends.

And Manfred here, that's what I call him, Manfred, was in a cage and for sale."

"Fascinating. He truly is an amazing creature. I can see why you'd want to purchase him."

"Are you sure you're all right, Chester?"

He hadn't moved an inch since Miss Stander revealed Manfred.

"Mm-hmm."

I didn't believe him. Though felines don't sweat, I could have sworn that Chester had water beading at his brow from his concentrated effort to remain calm and civil.

Missus Book thought it better to keep the conversation going while the wily little thing bounced about on the table. Perhaps by engaging in conversation, Chester might have an easier time keeping his thoughts away from murder. "He is amazing, to be sure. Is he a talking mouse?"

"I must say I don't know. He hasn't said a peep, but that's not to say he's not a talking mouse."

It was then I thought to interject my comments, "I've met many a talking animal and many that never utter a word, but it's my considered opinion that all the animals in the world are talking animals, some of them are just too shy to say so. What do you think Chester?"

Chester eased up a bit. He was always pleased when he was asked for his opinion and this time was no exception. "Well, it's a well-known fact that all animals, human or otherwise, have the cerebral capacity for speech. But are there not humans that can't speak also? Is it a matter of choice? Or is there an underlying biological problem there? Who really knows?"

Chester served us that food for thought on a platter and, as I was about to offer another point, we were all distracted by an eruptive sound reminiscent of a cannon from my years in the trenches.

The sound startled poor Miss Stander so much that most of her iced tea ended up on the front of her dress and the wooden slats of the porch. "My heavens!"

Missus Book stood with a kerchief, doing her best to sop up the mess on Miss Stander's dress.

The sound rang out again and it was a trifle easier to pinpoint the direction of it. It was clearly coming for a northeasterly direction and for a moment I wondered if the city proper had a war declared on it by some unknown force. "Dear Lord. I wonder if we really are under attack."

We stood there for a full minute, waiting for the thunderous booming to come again, but it seemed to have subsided and things calmed down a bit. We all took our chairs once more and grabbed our drinks for sipping. The mint julep was quite refreshing.

"I wonder what it was," Miss Stander stated in a voice that matched her rattled demeanor.

"I'm sure it was nothing. The factory is in that direction, perhaps there was a problem there."

Another long draught of my mint julep was just what I needed to settle down from all the excitement and speculation, but Miss Stander's level of arousal shot right back up again. "Where did he... Where has it gone to?"

"What? Where has what gone to, Miss Stander?" I looked about and for the life of me couldn't imagine what she was missing.

She ducked her head beneath the table and got low to the floor, looking beneath the chairs. That's when I noticed what was missing from the table. It was her marvelous, two-headed, three-legged mouse, Manfred, that was gone.

Miss Stander stood then and it seemed obvious. Her face turned beet red and from her throat came a sound like a teapot boiling over. Her eyes rolled into the back of her head and she fainted, collapsing to the floor of her porch. There was the tinkling of broken glass as her iced tea shattered over the ground.

It was then that Missus Book and I looked over to our feline companion. Chester's cheeks pulled back and he flashed us a sly, sharp-toothed grin that dripped with guilt.

"What did you expect? I might be a talking cat, but I'm still just a cat."

Dallas is Where Hope Goes to Die

THIS IS A RUSH TRANSCRIPT. THIS COPY MAY NOT BE IN ITS FINAL FORM AND MAY BE UPDATED.

JIM KNIGHT, KNIGHT REPORT ANCHOR: Welcome to the Knight Report for February 18, 2024. Tonight, we'll be talking about the big vote today on Capitol Hill. Did the speaker get the numbers from her own party to end a filibuster? Or has she lost control of not just the moderates, but her own party. But first, we have Dr. Jonathon Prothero. He cured cancer but he's still controversial. Some say he stole their research and the vaccine he's planning on giving away for free should be theirs to sell, right after this commercial break.

[Pfizer Pharma]

[McDonalds]

[Knight Report Promo]

[Viagra]

KNIGHT: And we're back. Welcome to the Knight Report. Our first guest tonight is Dr. Jonathon Prothero. He single-handedly cured cancer and, in a stunning move, plans to offer the vaccine at low or no cost to every man, woman, and child who wants the inoculation. He's been called a modern day Jonas Salk, but in other circles, he's known as a thief. Before we bring the doctor on, we have two Knight Report regulars to discuss the debate. On one hand, we have Dr. Jacob Michelson, he runs the left-leaning "Center for Science in the Public Interest." And next to him, we have Rick Chambers of the Center for Democratic Policy, headquartered in Washington, D.C. Thank you for being here, gentlemen...

DR. MICHELSON: Thanks.

RICK CHAMBERS: Thank you, Jim.

KNIGHT: I want to start with you tonight, Rick, because I'm a little confused about this. Your organization has been one of the loudest voices in calling for the prosecution of the man who cured cancer.

CHAMBERS: Well, simply put, we're on the side of the property owners who all live in a society of laws. Dr. Prothero stole intellectual property that didn't belong to him. And, although his goal was admirable, he built the vaccine on research paid for by Pfizer.

KNIGHT: So, you think he should be held liable for the billions Pfizer is presumably going to lose by not being able to sell this formula?

CHAMBERS: Trillions--

KNIGHT: Trillions?

CHAMBERS: We're talking about the cure to cancer. People around the world would be willing to pay top dollar for what Prothero wants to give away for nothing. Quite frankly, it's criminal.

KNIGHT: Let me bring you into this conversation, Dr. Michelson. What do you think about that? Sure, he cured cancer, but he broke the law and hurt a lot of influential people doing it.

DR. JACOB MICHELSON: What's missing from this debate is that Dr. Prothero didn't actually steal anything. Pfizer filed a patent on a gene that is involved in cancer growth. It wasn't like he broke into the laboratory and stole three fourths of the formula and just finished it up and released it before Pfizer could. He funded his own research and found that the cure involved a certain gene set that Pfizer patented for use. This is a loophole in patent law we're been working hard to lobby congress to eliminate.

KNIGHT: So, he's like a modern day Robin Hood...?

MICHELSON: But as I've said before, he hasn't stolen anything.

CHAMBERS: That's a pretty backwards view of the situation, Jake. No matter how benevolent his goals were and how hard you and your liberal friends lobby congress to change the laws of ownership, the fact of the matter is that Pfizer owns the patent on the exclusive right to exploit anything that affects that specific piece of genetic material. Prothero stole the use of that patent, costing a major American corporation trillions of dollars. This is a grave crime of the highest order.

KNIGHT: Switching gears, Dr. Michelson, I'd like to ask you when this vaccine will hit the streets. When can I get mine? (laughs)

MICHELSON: Well, it's the position of our Center that the sooner the better. Unfortunately, Pfizer has filed injunctions in court against the manufacturers contracted to mass-produce the vaccine by Dr. Prothero. Though Dr. Prothero has been making small batches and has been taking them on the road with him to decry Pfizer's actions, which are deplorable at best.

CHAMBERS: Deplorable? Jake, let me ask you a question. If an intruder were on your property in the middle of the night threatening your loved ones, belongings, and livelihood, would you do anything you could to protect it?

MICHELSON: Of course I would, but that hypothetical situation simply isn't applicable here.

CHAMBERS: Sure it is. Property is property.

MICHELSON: That's ridiculous...

KNIGHT: Gentlemen, we're going to have to leave that right there for a moment. When we come back, we'll be talking to Dr. Jonathon Prothero about his miraculous cure for cancer, his status as a would-be Jonas Salk, and the very real idea that he's a thief who built his cure on the backs of others. That's next on The Knight Report.

[Burger King]

[Volkswagon]

[Walmart]

[Pfizer]

KNIGHT: Welcome back to the Knight Report. Right now, we're going to be talking with Dr. Jonathon Prothero, the modern day Jonas Salk, the man who cured cancer and wants to give away the cure for nothing. He's also being called a monster, a liar, and a thief by the pharmaceutical industry. Dr. Prothero is joining us from our studios in Dallas, Texas. Welcome, Doctor...

DR. JONATHON PROTHERO: Thank you, sir. I'm happy to be here speaking with you.

KNIGHT: So, let's get to the meat and potatoes here, doctor. You've done a remarkable thing, but people are calling you names, saying that you're a thief, that you've stolen a piece of your cure. They say it's great you're giving away a piece of the pie, but you're giving away a pie that isn't yours. What to do you have to say...how do you respond to that?

PROTHERO: It's absurd.

(silence)

KNIGHT: Ummm... Do you have anything to add to that?

PROTHERO: What's to add?

KNIGHT: Well, I think people are making some pretty heavy duty accusations about you and they deserve your take on it.

PROTHERO: My take? My take is that curing cancer transcends property rights. I don't rightly care what they've patented.

KNIGHT: You think curing disease transcends property rights?

PROTHERO: That's what I said. Would you like to talk about the actual cure?

KNIGHT: We can move onto the actual method you discovered after we get to the bottom of the issue that's at the heart of this debate.

PROTHERO: What debate? You've made this into a debate, not me. I cured cancer and all you can talk about is whether or not you think I did it properly. Is there an improper way to cure one of the most deadly and pervasive diseases in our world? That's not rhetorical, the answer is no. As far as I'm concerned, if you don't want to talk about the issue, you can all go to hell.

KNIGHT: You don't need to... Please... Dr. Prothero, please sit back down. Oh God...

(Gunshots, screaming)

KNIGHT: I think... Do we have anyone there? Bob? Bob? What's going on down there? Yeah. Yeah? Ladies and gentlemen, it is my sad duty to inform you that Dr. Jonathon Prothero has been shot outside of our studio in Dallas.

A Badge and a Gun

It was Timmy Johnson's eighth birthday and his badge and gun would be arriving by mail some time this afternoon. Everyone received a license to detain or kill evil-doers on their eighth birthday. Eight years old is what they called "an age of responsibility." It was supposed to keep everyone honest. That's what they said anyway. When they passed the legislation, those in favor of it asked their constituents, "Who in their right mind would commit a crime if they knew that every citizen around them over the age of eight was carrying a loaded firearm and duly obligated to dispense justice?"

To their credit, the majority of Americans held it in their hearts that this was both foolish and stupid. Sadly though, the majority of their elected officials were in support of the Mandatory Firearms Protection Act of 2081. The majority of Congressmen received money from their campaigns from the National Rifle Association. The National Rifle Association was a group of people, hundreds of thousands, maybe millions of them, who got together as often as they could to shoot guns and talk about how great it was to shoot guns and to talk about how sorry they would make anyone who wanted them to stop shooting guns or to take them away.

They were gun-crazy.

So, because of this minority of gun-crazed individuals with deep pockets, little Timmy Johnson would be receiving his badge and gun that very day.

Timmy couldn't wait. Although he couldn't wait, his mother, Helen, could. She wasn't very enthusiastic about all of this. She was one of those Americans that thought it was both stupid and foolish to give anyone a gun, let alone an eight-year-old child. She didn't like guns at all, even hers. She hid her pistol in her nightstand drawer, unloaded and in its holster, as often as she could. She did this despite the fact it was illegal.

Not carrying your Government Issue firearm and badge was an offense punishable by a one thousand dollar fine and up to ten years in jail.

Displaying a reckless disregard for the law, Helen cooked a large, hot breakfast for her family without the aid and comfort of her gun. As her husband arrived at the table with his morning paper she was laying out this feast of pancakes and eggs and hash browns and bacon and French toast and milk and orange juice and coffee. Fred Johnson had stopped arguing with his wife about the bad example she set, vis-à-vis her gun. He'd given up threatening to report her a long time ago.

Sitting down with a sigh, he folded his newspaper around to the third page. "War, war, war. That's all they seem to print these days and I'm tired of reading about it..."

"Well, you know, dear," Helen offered after she set down a skillet of crispy bacon, "that's what's going on in the world."

"Mm-hmm..." He ignored her and continued reading between bites of breakfast and gulps of coffee.

The next to sit down at the table was Billy, Timmy's older brother. Both he and his father were wearing their pistols in leather shoulder holsters. Billy had received his gun in the mail four years prior on his eighth birthday. He still had four more years until he could get behind the wheel of an automobile.

"Morning, Mom. Morning, Pop."

"Good morning, Billy," his mother echoed.

Fred merely nodded, then added, "Hmmm..."

"Billy, be sure to say Happy Birthday to your brother. He's terrified you'll forget."

Exasperated, Billy rolled his eyes. "Mo-o-o-m... How could I forget? It's all he's been jawin' about for the last three months."

"I know, I know. But I'm your mother, dear. I worry about things like that. And I worry sometimes that you aren't good enough to your brother."

"He's lucky I ain't shot 'im."

Helen dropped a bowl of pancake batter on the floor, her face instantly streaming tears of appalled shock. These words out of her eldest sons mouth cut her deeply. "William Leroy Johnson, don't you dare say something like that. You promised me you'd never say such things."

"But, I got a right to, if'n..."

Fred interceded, cutting Billy off, "William. Listen to your mother. I've had plenty of reasons to shoot you, but have I?"

Red with shame and staring at his plate of hash browns, Billy allowed only two words to squeak out: "No, Dad."

"That's right. It's because I'm your father and I love you. And you should love your brother the same way."

"I know, I know..."

"I don't want to hear anymore about shooting your brother again. How can I enjoy my paper if you keep scaring your mother half to death?"

Helen had begun cleaning the pancake batter pooled on the floor. She sopped the mess up, muttering to herself after each teary sob, "Stupid... foolish... guns... all of them... they're just babies..."

She stopped every few moments to wipe the tears from her eyes.

Shooing his mother's sentiment away with his arm, Billy told his mother to hush up.

"Talk to your mother like that again and I will shoot you, son. And I'll have just cause to do it, too." Fred folded his paper over, becoming interested in an article about a twenty foot wall that had been erected between his country and his country's neighbor to the south.

When Timmy entered the room, wearing pajamas that made him look like his favorite super-hero, Helen did everything she could to hide the tears, but to no avail.

"Happy Birthday, Timmy," was all she could eke out between heavy breaths.

Fred folded his newspaper over again, this time flopping it onto the table. He offered his son a birthday tiding as well, "You're a big man now, Timothy. Eight years old."

Begrudgingly, Billy said, "Happy Birthday."

Timmy wiped the sleep from his eyes and yawned. "Is all this breakfast for me?"

Helen responded to this, "For your birthday, sweetheart."

"Is it here yet?" The excitement in Timmy's voice was unmistakable.

"No, Timmy, It'll be here sometime later." Helen was in no condition to answer this. Fred did, "You know how rare it is for the postman to arrive before you go to school."

Helen cried, "My babies..."

She turned her back to the family, hiding her tears and disgust for the idea that her eight-year-old son would, within hours, be a gun-toting time bomb, ready to kill at a moments notice.

"Oh, man... I was hoping I could take it to school so I could show Brad." Brad was Timmy's best friend at school. Brad had his pistol sent to him on his birthday about three months ago and had spent the time between then and now lording it over Timmy.

But the doorbell rang.

"Who could that be?" Fred wondered this aloud.

He got up to answer the door, but Timmy was off like a shot.

"It's the postman!" Timmy shouted to his family who was trying to catch up with him. Everyone but Helen ran to the door.

She remained in the kitchen to weep.

"Is there a Timothy Johnson here?" The postman was dressed quite officially with a big ribbon on his chest under his badge and an old fashioned six-shooter in a shoulder holster.

Timmy's eyes grew wide when he noticed the butcher-paper wrapped package under his arm. "It's me! It's me! I'm Timmy!"

With a paternal chuckle, the postman bent down to one knee and handed Timmy the package. "Well, young sir, I have a very important and special delivery here for you."

"It's here! It's here!" That was all Timmy could think to say.

"This package I'm delivering you is a very solemn thing. And I need you to sign this paper before you open it or carry your gun." The postman handed Timmy a clipboard and a pen. On the clipboard was a statement of responsibility.

Timmy let his box fall to one side, grabbing the clipboard and pen. "What's it say?" He scratched his head with the pen.

"It says you'll be careful with your gun, not take it out unless it's necessary and that you'll use it if you have to." The postman had become a more important aspect of daily life in America when the postal service was given the task of ensuring that everyone who had attained the age of eight received their badge and gun.

The postman was looked up to and respected once again.

"All right..." Timmy signed the document in his best penmanship, though even his best was scraggly and uneven.

The postman stood up, taking his clipboard back. With a chuckle he mussed Timmy's hair. "Just in time to show your pals at school."

The postman tipped his cap to Fred and said good day.

Timmy closed the door and ran straight to his bedroom, both to get ready for school and to strap his pistol to his belt. "Oh boy, oh boy."

The thought of his boy all grown into a man now forced Fred to get a bit misty eyed. Billy was a little jealous that he was no longer the only Johnson child in the neighborhood with his own gun.

Helen tried to compose herself enough to watch Timmy go to school, firearm strapped to his hip, but couldn't quite contain herself.

"It's okay, mom," Timmy tried consoling her. "I'm just going to school. I go to school every day."

"It isn't that, sweetheart..."

"What is it then, mom?"

"Just be careful with that... that..." She choked on her words...

"My gun and badge, mom?"

She burst into tears all over again. She kissed him on the cheek, told him she loved him and he was on his way to his second-grade classroom.

* * *

Timmy thumbed the hammer on his gun a hundred times on the school bus. He uncocked the hammer as many times.

He couldn't wait to show Brad.

Recess was the only time they were allowed to see each other because they'd been put in different classes this year.

Recess came quickly enough. Fifteen minutes of largely unsupervised bliss.

A little over two-thirds of the children on the playground had a loaded firearm strapped to his or her shoulder or belt. Timmy Johnson was now one of them. It made him feel good.

"Timmy!" Brad spotted him and called out his name in his high-pitched, prepubescent voice.

"Brad!" Timmy shouted back. "I got my badge today. My gun, too!"

They met under the monkey bars, as they did every day, and crouched in the woodchips, showing each other their guns. "These are so cool."

"Did the postman make you sign that paper?"

"Yeah."

"Mine, too. Did your dad show you how to clean your gun?"

"Not yet. I got it right before school, though."

"I bet he'll show you how to clean it after school."

"I bet."

Brad raised Timmy's pistol at arms length, getting a feel for its weight and aim. He pretended to target children on the other side of the playground.

"Wow."

"Mrs. Ulnick taught us about the cowboys in the wild west today and how they used to duel at high noon."

"Oh yeah?" Timmy felt Brad always knew more about everything than he did.

"Yeah."

"What'd they do?"

"Well, they'd start back to back and they'd count ten paces and then turn and shoot. Then whoever was left standing, won."

"Why did they do that?"

"That was how people settled things. Arguments and stuff like that."

"Wow."

"Yeah. Pretty cool, huh?"

"Yeah."

Across the playground, a fight erupted between two kids. Timmy recognized them as being fifth-graders. They were shoving each other and throwing sand at each other and hitting and kicking each other. Each had a gun strapped to his hip.

"We should stop 'em." Timmy didn't like to see people hurting each other.

He was a good kid.

"Yeah." Brad didn't like seeing people hurt each other either. But Brad had an idea. "I know what we can do."

Soon, Timmy and Brad had broken up the fight and explained to the fifth graders how they used to settle fights like men in the old west. A pair of children that young could only respond to such a romantically barbaric notion in one way: "Sounds like a good idea to me."

The older fifth-grader said that. He had dirt from his altercation smeared down one side of his face like chocolate. A bird could have easily nested in his curly locks of hair with the amount of twigs and bits of grass that were tangled in it.

"Me, too," the other fifth-grader agreed. His nose was broken and had a brownish crust of blood covering most of his upper lip.

"Timmy and I can be your seconds."

"Seconds?" asked the older one.

"We'll stand by you. I think that's what they do." Brad wasn't exactly sure, but it sounded good. "Yeah. We'll stand by you."

"We'll stand where you're supposed to turn and shoot. I guess." Timmy was getting excited to see this happen.

Brad set the fifth-graders back to back. He and Timmy stood next to them and carefully counted ten paces. They turned to face the quarrelling pair.

"All right!" Brad shouted, "This is where you'll shoot. I'll count to ten, then I'll call out to turn and fire."

"Okay." Both fifth-graders shouted in unison.

"They were both sweating and caressing the handles on their pistols with excitement and dread.

"One!"

They took a step at Brad's command. Then two.

Soon five and six and so on.

"TEN!"

There they stood. Twenty paces apart, backs turned. The anticipation was brewing. The gathered crowd, half a dozen students, was frenzied with curiosity and fright.

"Turn and FIRE!"

* * *

Helen was the only one home. Fred was at work and the children were still at school. She was putting together a shopping list in the pantry when a loud knock at the door startled her.

"Mrs. Johnson?" came a muffled voice from the other side of the door.

Helen asked herself who in the world that could be and put her list down on the table, heading for the door.

She opened it, not looking at who it was...

"Can I help you?"

She gasped when she realized it was a Public Safety Officer. He had two partners with him. All three were dressed in Kevlar armour and riot helmets. They wore black from head to toe, except for their shining, gold law enforcement badges.

"Mrs. Johnson?"

"I'm Mrs. Johnson."

"We might want to talk about this inside."

"Talk about what?"

"Inside, ma'am. Please. For your safety."

Helen's mind raced with the possibilities of what could bring them here at this time of day. Someone must be hurt or in trouble. A gnawing pit at the bottom of her stomach caused a pain so sharp it forced the breath from her.

She was frozen.

"Ma'am?" He had to repeat himself twice before she let them in.

"Of course."

They followed her to the living room. Helen couldn't bring herself to sit until the lead officer told her to. She was so nervous she would have smoked two cigarettes at once if she were prone to smoking at all.

"What... What is this about?"

"Well, ma'am. There's been an accident."

"An accident?"

"Yes. An accident. And before I tell you what happened I want to inform you that this sort of thing happens every now and again. There's nothing to be done about it. It's just one of those things."

"One of those things?"

"Yes, ma'am. One of those things."

The dread filled her belly with warm worry and crept up her face, making her ears hot and red.

"Well..." She couldn't remember what she wanted to say, so she said this instead, "why don't you sit down before you tell me what happened."

"I'd rather stand, ma'am."

"Mm-hmm..."

"You are Helen Johnson, correct?" She nodded in the affirmative. "And you are the mother of one Timothy Johnson, correct?" Again she nodded.

Tears appeared in her eyes, but the moisture clung to them. They couldn't decide if they should roll down her cheek or not yet.

"It is my duty to inform you that your son has been shot and killed in a minor firearms accident."

She was in shock. The officer doubted she heard what he'd just said, so he repeated himself. "Ma'am. I regret to inform you that your son is dead. There were shots fired in his playground at school. He was killed in the crossfire."

He wondered if she was going to say or do anything.

"I'm very sorry for your loss, ma'am."

Her focus suddenly snapped to the officer's eyes. They locked gazes. He could see the rage in her, welling up like a spring.

"Ma'am."

"You..." She said this calmly. None of the officers could have expected what happened next. "You bastards killed my boy!"

She was hunched over now.

Crying.

Hard.

"We didn't, ma'am."

"You killed him..." she fell to her knees and began pounding the officer in the waist, holding on to him.

"Ma'am, you're hysterical."

She pounded harder and harder, then screamed, "Why? Why did you do this to me?"

The officer backed up and drew his own pistol. "Ma'am, you're hysterical. One more move and I'll be forced to shoot."

"God-damn you and your guns!"

She was shrieking now, no discernible words left her lips.

Standing up, she lunged at the officer.

He fired four rounds into her body before she hit the floor.

"We better go report this."

The officer standing behind him, watching the whole thing, shook his head. "You think they wouldn't do this..."

The third cop was a little surprised. "This has happened before?"

"All the time."

"Seems like more and more people just don't know how to handle themselves."

The man who shot her looked down, examining the body. "She wasn't wearing her badge and gun, either."

"No wonder she attacked you like that, she was crazy to begin with."

"Mm-hmm..."

And they left to report this. They left Helen lying on the floor and paid Fred a visit at work to tell him about the tragic deaths of his wife and youngest son.

To them, it was business as usual.

An Evening of Cthulhu

My name is Phillip Quillan and I used to be a police officer in my day and, as they say, every dog has one. Before we continue further, a few things should be noted. First, the fact you're reading this means that I have passed on for reasons that will most likely forever remain my own. I have requested this be published posthumously.

Secondly, no matter how ludicrous or completely untrue any of this sounds, take heart that it is the absolute truth.

Finally, whenever possible, I've corroborated the facts and incidents with the diaries and the enumerating parties involved in this eerie situation.

We begin on August 1, 1949, in the diary of Elizabeth Shumway:

> I saw "it" today. I don't know what "it" was, but it was absolutely horrid. I'm not sure how my sanity was kept after this, this thing, came after me. It stood about two and a half meters tall and had deep red eyes. He was drooling, I think, and that translucent goo covering...dripping from his teeth was all that was visible. But in the dark of the alley it was in, I could hardly even make that out. Dear God, I beg of you, rid the world of this beast or I will die trying to do it myself. Why anyone would create such a horrid thing, I don't know. Deep down some part of me has to know why, but even thinking of it makes me nauseous.

What Elizabeth truncated from her entry was so startling when I first heard of it, that I could not understand how she could sit still long enough to vow her vengeance against this unholy creature.

But the story I discovered was so horrifying and otherworldly I can barely find words to describe it:

The bar they'd been enjoying themselves at was a good mile from their middle class apartment and it was quite unusual that two single sisters could find good enough jobs to support their lifestyle as well as pay for outings to the local swing scene.

It was well past two o'clock in the a.m. when they'd left, but it was well after sunrise before Elizabeth got to that apartment.

They walked home, like most would do, but this night…this night was different. The freshest of air was dank, musty and humid. It was enough to make one sweat with only the slightest effort. The night, however, remained in temperature an even 71 degrees Fahrenheit, enough to make a spine shiver easily.

In order for Elizabeth and her sister to reach their sparsely decorated domicile, they had to traverse through a labyrinth of dark, unforgiving streets and alley ways, all wet from a recent rain. The potholed pavement was stereotypically pockmarked with shallow reflecting pools.

The two were, understandably, slightly inebriated as they danced and skipped through the puddles, humming Benny Goodman tunes and giggling sporadically like schoolgirls. They were, after all, sisters who enjoyed themselves and the company of each other.

A slight fog rolled into the streets as they hopped along, not realizing the danger that awaited them.

It came from the night and disappeared back into it just as quickly. But for Elizabeth and her sister, not quick enough.

The beast came without a sound, but at the sight of the girls, it began to moan deeply with a thick timbre like a lion. It's eyes: the color of stoplights; it's teeth: moist and gnashing.

His–hers–it's body was sheer bulk and the sight of it sobered both girls swiftly. "R-r–run...Now–Go!" her sister shouted.

"Not without you." Elizabeth was quite stubborn in a tight spot and glanced about in a panic, looking for a formidable weapon to use against their nocturnal predator. Quickly, she located a discarded two-by-four and flailed it wildly at the beast. With one simple whip of its tail, the thing knocked Elizabeth against the alley's red brick wall. The two-by-four went skittering across the damp ground with a dog-like snarl from the demon.

For the demon, he thought only to hurt other things, but on the same token, to offer itself joy and pleasure.

He grabbed Elizabeth's sister with his clawed hand and placed her legs in his mouth, one at the hip and the other at the knee. If you've ever seen a puppy shake it's stuffed prey as soon as it sinks its teeth, then you know what happened to Elizabeth's sister.

Unfortunately for her, a puppy doesn't have teeth that could crush, slice and mash flesh and bone. The creature did. After a shake of its head or two, her right leg at the hip and her left at the knee, were a bloody pulp the creature worked hard to sluice between the razor-edges of his teeth.

It threw her and she hit the wall, and then the ground, like a rag doll.

Her screams filled the night and the creature fled back into it, from whence it came.

I don't know why the thing attacked them, and I don't know why it happened to these two young girls. What I did know was that I was tired and had no knowledge of the unholy goings-on. At least not enough to investigate properly. I slept.

For Elizabeth and her sister, however, the rest of the night they spent in the hospital, being cared for by an ex-army field-medic-turned-grave-shift-emergency-surgeon. Elizabeth would survive the attack with minor cuts and bruises, her sister though, would spend the rest of her life in a wheelchair.

You might stop to ask yourself now why I'm writing this and, for the most part, I don't know. What I do know is that this story simply must be told and, though I'm now presumably dead, I'm the one to tell it.

I only wish I had time to finish it.

Convention Sketches

From the moment he stepped out onto the pavement in front of the transit station he was clearly lost. He tapped out the address to the hotel into his phone with one hand and guarded his luggage warily with the other, but to no avail. Confusion washed over his face like a cold sweat and it was apparent to everyone.

"Which hotel you lookin' for?" A voice called out from the void.

"Huh?" He looked around, wondering where it came from.

"Which hotel you tryin' to get to?" the voice asked again, revealing itself as a lanky black man in an oversized T-shirt.

"Ummm... The Marriott." The nerd replied, unsure of himself, his voice breaking.

"You here for the Con, right?"

"Yeah."

"Shit, man, I could tell jus' by lookin' at 'ya."

"Really?"

"Yeah, man, come on, the hotel's this way."

And without a second to think better of it, the pair of them were off on their way.

"Shit, man, the look on your face, I thought you were stayin' at some place way out of town, but your place is close, man."

"Oh, yeah?"

"Yeah, man. So you ready to party?"

"Ummm..."

"You ever been to this Con, man?"

"No. This is my first time."

"Shit, man. This place is a par-tay. You guys for the con really know how to party, like, it doesn't stop, man."

"You here for the Con?" he asked, naively.

"No, man. I'm homeless. I work the conventions now and again setting stuff up, but mostly I'm just homeless."

"Oh."

"This place is always better when the Con is goin' on, though."

"Con's are a lot of fun."

They reached the intersection and the homeless man pointed down the street to the right. "Down that way, that's where the party is all the time. That restaurant, it don't close. There's a party going on there from tonight through the weekend, it's fuckin' kickin'."

He pointed down the left, "Now we're gonna cross down this street, and then your hotel is gonna be right here close. C'mon."

And they went as soon as the light changed.

"So, man. This is it. This is you right here, man. You just head up that walkway there and you at the Marriot lobby. It'll be a party in there all weekend, too, for sure."

"Thanks for the help, man."

"No sweat, man. But now that I helped you, you think you can help me out, like help me get something to eat tonight?"

"For sure," he said and without thinking his wallet was out and he had a crisp five dollar bill in his hand.

He gestured for the homeless man to take it.

"For reals?"

"Of course."

Thankfully, he snatched the bill and offered his hand for a shake. "Shit, man. You're all right. My name's Sylvester."

He took his hand and shook it with gusto. "Andrew."

"Andrew, you should come on down and hang out tonight, man. You're all right."

"Maybe. I don't know what's going on."

"For sure."

"But seriously, thanks for your help. I really appreciate it..."

"My pleasure, man. My pleasure."

They shook hands again and parted ways, never to see each other again. Andrew left thinking, I feel like that was money well spent, what a way to start a con, and he meant it.

* * *

Of the forty years of the San Diego Comic-Con, Gerald had been to the last twelve, and of the last four, he'd been the proud retailer in booth 1216 who specialized in rare, vintage comics. When he arrived at the convention center on Monday, the exhibition hall seemed deep, dead, and empty. Pallets of materials stood in the center of the carpeted off areas, leaving no hint or promise of what fascinating attraction they might become.

Monday was always spent assembling his makeshift storefront: walls of thin black grating, a table with a white linen cover and a trio of bookshelves that needed assembly to serve as the back wall. This would be his temporary home for the next week. Tuesday was spent rifling through the inventory he'd brought, hefting and sorting long box after long box full of the kind of comics that had brought him joy over his forty-three years of life.

He spent Wednesday putting comics up for display on the shelves and walls. A Stan Lee Daredevil. A Bob Kane Batman. Spider-man. Superman. The Hulk. The Flash. On and on and on and on.

The last comic to find its way onto the display wall was Gerald's favorite book, the first one he'd ever acquired to resell. It was an extremely well preserved copy of the first issue of The X-men from 1963. Through the plastic clamshell, one could see the sharp corners and vivid colors with the first Jack Kirby rendering of what would become one of the most iconic rivalries in modern history: Magneto versus the X-Men.

He'd tried selling it in the past, but it was never in extraordinarily high demand at a show like this, and for the price he was selling it for. He secured it to the metal lattice of his wall with a plastic zip tie at each corner, and at eye level, so he could glance at it periodically through the day. It would calm him in a way, from the overwhelming nature of the show.

5:30 on Wednesday, the exhibition floor was ready, the doors would be opened, and thousands of four day pass holders would get their first glimpse of the hall, spilling into each aisle, elbow to elbow, a sea of sweaty geeks who had spent all day in line for their passes and then admittance.

Business was always slow for Gerald on Preview Night. The Hall was open only for three hours and the majority of people were on the floor merely to collect swag. At least that's how it seemed to Gerald. People who stopped by on the first night were there to gawk or browse. For many of those passing by, it was their first in-person encounter with Amazing Fantasy #15, or Detective Comics #27, or whatever. Sometimes, a father would stop with his eight year old son and point to an issue on the wall and say, "That was the first comic book that Wolverine was ever in," or, "That issue of Secret Wars, yeah, the orange one, that was the first Venom costume ever." It would fill Gerald with a hopeful satisfaction knowing that he was a torch bearer for an art and medium that was important. At the end of the day he was a purveyor of history and culture, "And that," he'd always add, pointing at his prized issue of The X-men, "Is the first time The X-men ever appeared, and they were already fighting Magneto from the start."

Things picked up on Thursday and Friday, but Saturday was always the biggest, busiest day of the Con.

Saturday was the day everyone attended. It was impossible to breathe for all the people crammed into each aisle. Traffic would invariably congest right in front of Gerald's booth every few minutes when someone would catch sight of a rare comic book that was their hearts desire. It was at that moment Gerald would swoop in. "Wanna see it up close?" he'd ask, always knowing the answer.

He'd be reaching for it before they would have a chance to respond. He could see them straining their eyes for a glimpse at a price tag or marker, and it would always make him chuckle just a bit. He never put a price on it. Not because he thought the asking price would scare people away too much, but because he wanted an excuse to pull it off the shelf and talk to people about it.

It would take a moment for him to loosen the straps that bound it to the wall, but it would always be worth it. Handling it gave him an inexplicable rush.

The sea of backpacks and costumed superheroes was overwhelming by midday. People lapped up on the shore of his booth, interest in his wares waxed and waned with the ebbing tide of potential customers.

Soon, a man arrived carrying a metal attaché case, placing it on the table in front of Gerald. Attache cases always meant business. Gerald knew this game and asked him, "You buying or selling?"

"Buying. Buying plenty."

Gerald rolled up his sleeves, getting down to business. He was a very focused man and quite honestly didn't see anything else when he was making a deal.

"What is it you'd like, and what is it you're interested in paying?"

"Well, I'm looking for four key issues, and I've been told you're the man to see."

"I may well be, what can I help you find?"

"First and foremost, I'm looking for a Hulk #181, Giant-Size X-Men #1, Uncanny X-Men #130 and, surprisingly, #1."

"Well, #130's are dime a dozen, what is that, Dark Phoenix?"

"First appearance of Dazzler. I've got a client and he wants first X appearances. He's a celebrity, wants to remain anonymous."

"I've got a Giant Size here..." Gerald turned and reached down deep into a box and withdrew a clam-shelled copy of the seminal issue. "Hulk #181 is a little harder. That would take some doing. I can't think of anyone here at the show who has one. If you give me a week, I can probably track one down, probably for about half of what you can get it for on eBay."

"And Uncanny #1?"

"You're in luck, friend." Gerald turned to his happy place...to see nothing but a blank space on the wall.

The blood drained from his face.

"You okay?" the would-be buyer asked Gerald.

"Ummm..."

Gerald looked around, trying to see where it could have gone.

"I'll come back," the buyer said as he slid his business card across the table while sliding his attaché case off.

Gerald rose from his stool, not even noticing the customer fleeing. Could he have been responsible? No. That was absurd.

Suddenly, it seemed as though each passer by was a suspect. Could it have been the pimple-faced teenager with the green backpack, the Thor with the bad wig, the overweight Deadpool? Panicked, Gerald went back to the wall, inspecting the ties he'd so carefully unbind each time he pulled it down to see that they'd been cut.

Slowly, it hit him like a kick in the chest.

His book was gone.

Never to return.

He slumped back onto his stool, defeated. His posture left him, he was hunkered down as though his spine was giving out. Someone had just walked off with thousands of dollars worth of one comic book.

Gerald buried his head in his hands and wondered quietly where he would get the strength and inspiration to carry on for the rest of the show.

* * *

The most fascinating moment from the Con was my encounter with perhaps the most socially awkward and retarded human being the world has ever known. There I was, standing next to a friend at an exhibitors booth on the dealer room floor where we were both admiring items we wanted to purchase as much as the reasonably attractive young lady who was helping us. She was blonde, freckled and of a slight frame. Her face was plain but cute and she wore a tight black corset that created a mesmerizing effect with her bosom. In short, she was beautiful.

"I want to get it," my compatriot told her, of the overpriced Darth Vader snow globe she'd pulled down from the top shelf for him to look at.

"And I'd like to get this," I added, indicating the shirt I wanted from the table.

"All right, let me find out how much with tax," she told us in her faux-British accent, no doubt practicing for some Renaissance fair or another.

"Ummm..." A voice interrupted our transaction, clearly begging for her attention.

"Yes, can I help you?" she asked the boy politely. Though "boy" may be a misnomer, the unkempt, mouth-breathing "boy" was easily in his mid-twenties.

"Yes, I would like to know how much that Musha Cloth Heavy Weapons Gundam behind you is," he said in a voice that was stereotypically nerdy: nasally and unsure despite the matter-of-fact tone. He pointed at a massive gray and red box behind her that looked like it could fit four or five board games inside of it.

"That's $230," she told him quickly, "would you like to see it?"

"No. I have a friend who has one. He already built it, I know what it's like."

"Uh-huh," she said as we emptied money from our wallets to make our purchases.

"I think I might get it. My parents owe me the money." It seemed painfully obvious he wanted to impress her with his story, but to what end we couldn't be sure.

"Oh," she replied, trying to pay attention to our transaction, and not him.

"You see, I need to babysit my grandfather this weekend and they owe me money for that," he continued his intended courtship.

She nodded at him, still calculating tax for our items.

"He's 94."

I suppressed a laugh, realizing that this was about as bad things could get for this poor kid. At least that's what I thought.

"He's incontinent and doesn't like to wear adult diapers."

My companion and I shared a wide-eyed look as our cashier blushed badly, trying her hardest to make eye contact with us and not the boy. And just as I thought things couldn't get worse, the boy opened his mouth again.

"Somebody has to clean up that mess. And they pay me to do it." Completely disarmed, her hands dropped to her side, unable to concentrate on her customers.

"Yeah," the unfortunate boy continued, "I've already spent $400 at this con. I think I'll get that Gundam. I just need to ask my parents. Maybe I'll be back."

"Okay," the poor girl said, sheepishly, as he walked away without a graceful goodbye of any sort.

After holding our breath for fear of laughing, finally the dam broke. "Wow," my companion said after bursting into torrent of laughter. "You know where I come from," he told the girl, "when you want to impress a pretty girl, there are a lot better ways to do it."

Her face was flushed and red, her eyes were darting about, not sure of herself. She laughed nervously, trying to let some of the emotion escape.

Finally, I asked her, "Does, uh, that happen to you often?"

"I don't think anyone has ever tried to impress me by talking about poop."

The tension broke as she said it and we all broke out into a deep and hearty laughter over the whole episode. Once the laugh was over, we completed our intended task, I stuffed my new shirt in my bag and we walked away, wondering how the awkward boy felt about his top game in attracting girls.

Battle Drone Six

Every other combat mission briefing I'd been party to had been dripping with a sense of dread, as though the humidity was infused with terror. This one was different, though. There were a dozen of us, all grunts, all very young, and all sitting in front of a computer running a dormant video game.

The video game looked like any other first person shooter I'd ever played in my life.

Our commanding officer was a gruff old man with a white mustache and I had always imagined that he would have fit in the military better in 1940 than now. He just had that look about him, like he would rather be wearing aviator glasses, an old crush cap, and be gnawing on the end of a corn cob pipe.

He stood at the head of the room in front of a massive multi-screen array that was currently showing a map of an insurgent camp in primary colors. I could only assume we'd be doing a simulation on the layout of that typical village.

A simulation was the only thing I could guess based on our orders. We were to report here for a confidential briefing at 1900, and there was no need for our kit.

"You're all here because you've been handpicked for this operation. You've all got good heads on your shoulders, you've all got plenty of combat experience and I'm told you all like your video games. Team oriented first person shooters is your poison, from what I hear. As you saw in your orders, this operation is classified as Top Secret. We will not be discussing it outside of this room for any reason."

This was starting to sound serious, for a simulation at least.

"You will all be controlling, via the control station in front of you, a battle drone. You're each networked to a field tested robot that has been dropped into position around this hot zone, here."

On the screen, a perimeter around the village lit up. We'd be on the outskirts moving in. The view zoomed in and rotated, revealing dots numbered one through twelve. Each of our computer systems was numbered accordingly.

I was designated as number six.

"The name of this village is need-to-know, but it's one that has a major insurgent presence. General Wakefield estimated casualties for a traditional incursion at well over a hundred. With our intelligence and these experimental drones, we will eliminate opposition in this key area with a zero percent chance of losing one of our own."

I grinned.

Easily the worst part of these raids was watching your friends and comrades die, or discovering that they hadn't made it back after the fact. Taking all the emotional weight out of the equation made this seem like it could actually be fun.

I never thought I'd think of making war as fun. It's a dangerous thing.

"The interface has been designed to emulate popular first person shooting games. You will have a chance before we go live to configure your controls. As a word of warning: these machines are highly advanced and based on experimental technology. We cannot allow them to fall into enemy hands. These machines can take quite a beating, but if their structural integrity falls below a certain threshold, down to zero from one hundred on your heads-up-display, they will self destruct, causing a radius of considerable damage."

He checked his watch and explained to us our objectives. We'd be entering the city and securing a building in the town square where insurgent leaders were believed to be in the basement, plotting their vicious schemes. "Standard orders of engagement apply. This is a small village and there are any number of potential civilians that can get in the way so be sure to check your targets. You are authorized to eliminate insurgent threats with prejudice.

"As I said before, you've been selected for your predilection to video games, so I doubt you'll have any problems configuring your controls. We go operational at 1930. Good luck and godspeed."

The station in front of me was just like any computer I'd ever used. I set my controls the same way I'd done for every FPS I'd ever played.

My right hand on the mouse would be my eyes and sense of direction as well as my trigger finger. My left hand would rest casually on the keyboard, operating my locomotion, backwards and forwards, side to side, and I'd be able to reload or switch to other weapons with the touch of a button.

I'd played plenty of networked games in my day, and I wondered if the lag between my station here and the robot out in the desert would be a problem, but my thought was they wouldn't be having us try this if it hadn't be tested. Not on a target that seemed so vital, anyway.

What if we were the ones being tested, and the robots were just made up? What if this was all just a game the psych boys cooked up to test the effects this kind of technology would have on us? Let's be honest, robots connected to computers seemed like a substantial leap in technology. Anything was possible, though, so I'd just play things straight.

"By now, you've had time to acclimate yourselves to your controls. Be sure to adjust the volume on your headsets. The operation will be going live in three...

"Two...

"One..."

The screen went black and it seemed as though our robotic avatars were rising slowly out of the ground. My guess was that the battle drones were kept in capsules with sharp ends at the bottom so when they were dropped into a zone they'd be impacted underground until the operation went online.

After my drone had raised itself up to ground level, I was given control. I looked left and right, hoping to get a glimpse of a comrade. I was dying to see what one of these things looked like.

It was night, obviously, and the details were fuzzy so I switched to night vision and everything became a menacing shade of green. The drones looked very much like a linebacker in full pads made of three inch steel. The faces of the drones were an array of cameras and technology mounted above a thick grill where a mouth should be. Each of our steel monstrosities carried an M16, a pistol as a sidearm, a stash of grenades, and a long, carbon steel knife.

We could do an exquisite amount of damage with these Battle Drones. There was a spike of adrenaline in my blood when our commander interrupted our dallying, "We are on a timetable, gentlemen."

Each of the monitors on the array where he gave our briefing had turned into twelve miniature screens where he could watch over the entire mission and offer pointers. He was listening in on a headset and giving commands through a microphone.

His voice reminded me that I was treating this like a video game, but this was real. There were real lives at stake and live rounds in my firearms. I had to remind myself that firing my weapon in this game was, as far as I knew, the same thing as firing it in the field.

Through my headphones, I could hear the quiet sounds of the desert and the low, hydraulic hum of my robot, then the commanders voice cut in again. "Battle Drones Four through Six, form up and perform a sweep on the building to the north of your position.

"Copy that," we all said at the same time.

This really was a video game in every way. The camera movement was graceful and fluid, just like a game, and so it seemed like I was floating through the air instead of walking with a bobbing gait over the terrain.

Our detachment, Drones Four, Five, and Six, moved quickly to the back wall of the simple, stucco building and split up. We were looking for a point of ingress. I made my way around the right side of the building and they made their way around the left. The area was clear and we found a door on the far side.

"How do we open a door?" Five asked.

"I'll do it," I told them.

Jockeying myself in front of the door, I pressed the enter key. My robot reached out with his free hand and threw the door open.

They dove in, fingers on their mouse-button triggers, checking the room out. I turned, glancing around to make sure there weren't any enemies in the area opposite us that wanted to shoot at us, and headed into the building myself after hearing that the entry way was all clear.

Once inside, I could see that this building was one giant rectangular room that was furnished sparsely.

I would have liked to inspect the room in closer detail, for trap doors or hidden passages, but the interface simply wasn't capable of it. I wasn't even sure if the robot was capable of bending over to do as much. I knew the robot could crouch, but that was about it.

Doing our best to inspect what we could, we came back to the door after flagging the building as clear.

It seemed odd to me that there would be a completely vacant building on the outskirts of town, but it bolstered my theory about all of this being a simulation.

There was a crack like thunder in the air and I knew shots had finally been fired.

"There's a situation in the main square. Drones Three through Nine approach immediately with extreme caution." The commander's voice was still calm and collected.

We assembled at the door, which had closed behind us, and the tumult of the battle outside grew louder. There were three-round bursts of gunfire and shouting from other parts of the room that I couldn't hear through my headset.

I pressed enter and we could see the fiery battle going on in the village center. Insurgents were firing from the building interiors and rooftops and our compatriots were pinned to walls.

"Let's do this," Five said and he charged into battle at a sprint.

This was just a video game to him and he had no thought of the consequences.

Playing catch up, Four and I chased after him until a mortar of some type hit the ground between Four and me and our companion.

I turned, changing directions on a dime, strafing to my right and aiming up at the building I thought the mortar might have come from.

Seeing a figure on the rooftop, I tapped my mouse button twice, hurtling six armour-piercing rounds up at the attacker. He was hit and downed by at least one burst of fire and dropped down below the lip of the roof, obscuring him from my sight.

I ducked into the alleyway between two buildings less than fifty yards from the epicenter of the action.

"Four, get over here, I'll cover you." I whispered, forgetting that he could hear me plain as day in his head set and my voice would, more than likely, not be reproduced by the robot.

He got the idea and came in my direction. I checked the windows and rooflines, feeling hampered by my limited field of view that cut off my peripheral vision almost completely. Sure, I had an impressive high-definition wide screen display, but no matter how wide the screen was it couldn't reproduce the edges of the natural sight.

A human figure dashed between buildings across the street from me, and I tapped the mouse button, launching a barrage of shots at the target. Plaster exploded with the impact of my bullets, but they all hit so quickly, I couldn't tell if I hit my target at all, or just the plaster.

Four fell in behind me and assessed the situation.

There was a water well in the middle of the square and three of our mates were pinned down to the ground on the side of it closest to us. It was odd to see three figures crouching below the stone well, all of them in the exact same position. Every few moments, one of them would peek their head up over the lip of the well and fire a few rounds off toward the rooftops.

Five had disappeared from our view entirely. He could have been dead for all I knew.

"Five? Report your position."

Though I could hear his actual voice to the left of me, his radio distorted voice piped in through my headset. "I'm across the street. Can you see me? I'm directly across from you."

I wheeled my mouse around and shifted my field of view enough to see Five. I had my crosshairs on him in no time.

"What's the situation from that side?" I asked him.

"There's two on the roof above you, One, Two and Three, are there pinned under the well, and Seven, Eight, and Nine are two buildings in front of you. I have no fix on Ten through Twelve."

"Can you see any other hostiles?"

"Negative, but there is a lot of action coming from the buildings across the square."

"I can see that."

I strafed to my left, peeking my head around the corner, trying to see if I could get a bead on one of the hostiles pinning One through Three down. That's when things got sketchy.

Sketchy was putting it mildly.

There was a fizzing pop and then a trail of smoke flew from the rooftop above me and smashed into Two, ending in a bright flash of an explosion.

His structural integrity must have been low already because his armour made a horrible shrieking sound, like a fuse burning at an inordinately high pitch, right before it exploded into a stunning light that turned my screen bright white. I switched to my regular vision setting and could only make out broad strokes of the aftermath. Two's explosion had destroyed not just the well, but One and Three, also. They simply weren't there anymore, disintegrated into black spots of dirt.

Not having a target, I pulled back and looked to Five, who had opened fire on the targets above Four and me.

One of them fell down the front of the building and hit the cobblestone in front of me with a startling impact, blood spraying everywhere. If this was a video game, it had the most realistic renderings of blood, gore, and broken bodies that I had ever seen.

The combatant who'd fallen to the ground was a tangled mess of broken bones and raw meat, pouring blood out everywhere in ways that felt real.

Glimpsing movement in the distance I targeted and fired quickly. I was shooting into a group of terrorists, dropping two like sacks of potatoes.

Four came around my flank and joined in, dropping a third and fourth from the roof above.

At that point it became a free for all. Everyone ran into the fray. If they were on the run, we needed to press the advantage. Since we were safely in a command center operating these metal monsters, there was no fear of mortality. We reached that adrenal peak of activity you hit when you're playing a video game and we charged in.

After seeing what had happened to One, Two, and Three, we all decided to keep our distance from each other. It was unspoken between us, but that was the nature of war and video games: changing tactics in the face of the situation.

When I played games like this, my favorite thing to do was to find a back way to the action and outflank everyone while my comrades took the frontal assault, and when I saw everyone else going for the front, I realized this would be a perfect time for my flanking maneuver. Instead of charging forward with the rest of them, I reversed direction, came through the back of the alleyway and found myself sprinting behind the buildings. Knowing there were no friendlies near me, I opened fire at everything that moved. I tagged three bad guys with the tap of the mouse. A rushing feeling of dread filled me, as though I were getting away with something. Being sneaky in a game always had that effect on me.

On my way I could hear the chatter from my detachment.

"Two on the roof, 3:00."

"Taking fire from the right."

"Behind us!"

There were two explosions and the radio went silent. I knew I was the lone survivor from my squad.

I'd passed by three buildings from behind that had curved around and, by my estimates, seemed to put me in line past the fountain.

A hand on my shoulder startled me. It was the commanding officer. Apparently, I was the last one alive in this entire operation.

Hitting the control key, I set my robot to crouch in a bid to remain stealthy. Sneaking up the edge of the center plaza, I could see the scorched remains of the well and the last group of rebel fighters making their way to the square, prematurely celebrating their victory and looking for any signs of what it was that had just hit them.

Not wanting to accidentally fire and give away my position, I took my fingers off of the mouse buttons and began counting targets. It seemed as though no one was left in the city but the terrorists holding palaver in the town square.

It wasn't until a pair of them raised their weapons in the air and fired them, as if in victory, that I could reasonably assume that they were the last survivors in their cell.

There was a feeling of a crowd holding its breath behind me as I leveled my sights on the heads of the remaining soldiers and pulled the trigger, dragging my cursor over them each in turn.

There was only one left, but I was finally out of ammo. Consulting my heads up display, I still had eighty hits left and so I switched to my knife.

Pulling my headphones off, I took a deep breath. From the crowd behind me, I could hear a pin drop.

Holding down the shift and up-arrow keys, I stormed the lone enemy like a bull going in for a killing stroke against a matador.

He unloaded his clip into me, my hits were dropping faster than a hooker's panties, but I finally reached him, savagely plunging my knife into his face once, twice, four, six, eight times until his body collapsed to the ground.

He crumpled like paper and blood ran out of his head like maple syrup.

A cheer erupted behind me.

I glanced at my remaining life. It was a flashing, red fifteen percent.

"By the skin of my teeth."

I cracked my knuckles and stood, relieved that it had all been over.

But I wanted more.

To some degree I knew all well designed video games were addictive, but this might have taken the cake. The prospect that it might have been real was so alluring that I wanted to jump right back into it.

Our commander clapped his hand on my back in a congratulatory fashion before retaking his place back up on the dais.

He pressed a combination of buttons on his keyboard and I could see my screen counting down to a self-destruct, then it turned white, presumably from my battle drone's explosion.

It made sense, I guess. If these robots were real, they only had a one-way ticket, which was somehow sad because they must have been worth a fantastic sum of money.

"If you all would like to take your seats again, I'll be debriefing you."

We all did as ordered, excited about the promise of what this new technology had to offer.

If we could fight a war with nothing more than a network party, we wouldn't hesitate to launch an assault against anyone or anything. I couldn't decide if I was becoming more or less of a fan of this idea. On one hand, going on a mission like this would have all the dread of a pizza party and none of my friends would be put in harms way. On the other, would it make the act of making war so impersonal that we'll lose the gravitas required to conduct it?

Such heady philosophy wasn't for me to decide, I supposed, so I just sat at attention.

"The operation went smoothly, for the most part, but you all seemed to forget you weren't in a video game or a simulation and made some pretty glaring tactical mistakes."

He was right. We were playing as though we'd respawn as quickly as our virtual bodies hit the floor.

Instead, we were blowing up millions of dollars in taxpayer funds. Even trying to be conscious of it, it was hard for me to put myself into a headspace for self-preservation. In a video game, you're completely disposable because you're accustomed to coming right back to life seconds after you've died.

"In just a moment, we'll have some live boots on the ground in this sector with helmet-cams. They'll do a final sweep and we'll take a look at exactly what we did out there. I think we can be reasonably certain that we did all the hard work, though."

Slowly, the dozen screens behind the commander faded from static to the cameras of the clean up crew. The images came into focus in varying shades of green, white, and black.

As our boys on the ground moved into a position that would be a worthwhile vantage point, our commander continued the briefing.

"As I'm sure you've guessed, each of the drones were slated for destruction at the end of this operation. All of the data the boys in R and D would need was uploaded to their servers, and we recorded each of the individual video feeds. They'll be analyzing this whole operation, top to bottom, inside and out, for a long time to come. With any luck, we'll be able to conduct more operations in this fashion and we'll be able to save a significant amount of lives."

I suppose it all was real and for some reason that made me sad.

For the first time, it hit me that I had ended lives. They were the enemy, sure, and they'd have killed me without hesitation, but it's never a happy thing to take a life.

It marks you, somehow.

But I didn't know how hard it would be on me.

The cameras had approached the plaza where we'd had our final fight and the sight was familiar, but not recognizable. The hole of the well was there and so was the ground where One, Two, and Three had bought the farm. It was scorched and pockmarked.

"I don't think you're gonna believe this." That was a voice from the field. Presumably, the young soldier whose camera we were watching.

"What is that?" The commander raised his voice as though to make up the distance between us with force of volume alone.

The young soldier didn't respond.

He simply aimed his camera at the pile of bodies closest to the blackened piece of earth that I guessed was where my avatar self-destructed.

Out in front were the mutilated remains of the poor bastard I'd knifed in the face, but behind him were the stacked remains of a panicked family.

Murdered at the hands of Battle Drone Six.

At my hands.

Could it have been a trick of my eyes? Or a fuzzy signal? I wasn't the only one terrified about this prospect. The commander asked, "Foxtrot, copy?"

"Foxtrot, here."

"I'm going to need you to...get a closer look."

"Copy that."

Gun drawn, he stepped over to the bodies and crouched. Hesitantly, he kicked the ankle of the topmost corpse. We all startled as he jerked back.

The face was covered over completely by a burka and the body beneath was child sized.

My heart sank and my chest filled with bile.

I felt no better than if I'd have been there, pulling the trigger myself. But I guess I was there, tapping a mouse key, and by proxy pulling a trigger.

Actually, the more I chewed on it, the worse I felt. I had taken pleasure in this entire enterprise. And I did things I promised myself I'd never get wrapped up in.

We finished the debriefing, but I couldn't begin to tell you what was said.

I was somewhere else.

A million miles away, lost in myself.

I got to my bunk and spent a sleepless night tossing and turning, trying to make myself feel okay about what I'd been shown and what I'd done.

All it did was remind me that war is war. Here or there, from far away or right up in front of you, it all ends up the same way.

It all means the same thing, one incontrovertible truth: war is hell and that's a fact.

My Cross to Bear

Things had been bad for a long time for everyone, not just me. Everybody's got their own problems but I've got my own unique crosses to bear. I don't like talking about them, though, because that's always liable to cause more trouble than it's worth and it pretty much always ends up with me and my girl getting run out of town. Mostly, though, we keep to ourselves. We've got a room in the hotel right above the town saloon. That's where we spend our time and take our meals.

We don't talk much to strangers and other folk. I work hard enough for the both of us to keep us out of trouble. It's a rough life and plenty of hard work, but it's worth it because I love her so damned much, no matter what anybody says about people like her.

Problems always start when folks get nosy, and nosy is how things got that warm night that started with a dusty twilight.

"Welcome back, Mr. Remington," the saloonkeeper greeted me the same way every night. It didn't vary to the point where I felt like it was part of the routine.

"Howdy," I'd respond like a preprogrammed robot, and I'd just head up the stairs to my room to be with my Sylvia.

But it was then, on this blistering hot, fateful night, that the saloonkeeper stopped me, offering me a drink he'd already poured. "On the house, just hang about and chat with me for a few."

"Hang about and chat?"

"Well, you're always runnin' up to your room, barely sayin' hello-goodbye. You're a guest here and I feel like the better I know you, the more I can make you feel at home while you're stayin' here."

"That's awful nice of you," I accepted the drink, a dry rye whiskey, "but we're just quiet folk who like to keep to themselves. Being able to do that makes it home enough."

"Well, you know it's a small place and people get to talking."

"I'm not one for much talking, Mr. Witwer."

"I can see that. Two months here and we've spoken more to-night than in that whole stretch of time."

"I work hard and in the sun. Most days I don't rightly feel like talkin' afterwards."

"I hear that. Most times I get home after a long night here and I just button up tight and don't want to say word one to nobody."

"Mm-hmm." I swigged my drink and was just about to head upstairs to my beloved Sylvia when he said the one thing that could turn my head back to him and his damn fool conversation.

"Well, people been talking about your girl. They been wondering if she's all right in the head. It's mighty peculiar, not seein' her out of her room at all."

I stopped and stared, unsure of what to say. Invariably, it was this line of questioning that was the beginning of the end of my and Sylvia's time in a town, and as many times as I'd lived through it, I'd never come up with a right response. "Is that what they say?"

"People like to talk."

"I suppose they do, don't they? I can assure you, though, nothing's wrong with her, thank you very much."

"Well, I'm right sure there isn't anything wrong with her. If'n you say so, I'm on your side."

"Thank you for that, Mr. Witwer."

"But if you want the talk to stop, you might want to bring her down to the social tonight."

"The social?" Everything in my gut was telling me this would be an extraordinarily bad idea.

"Every once in a while, maybe every three or four months or so, the town council declares an evenin' holiday and we throw a social here in the saloon. Anybody who's anybody'll be here and I'd be right honored if you and your lady attended. When they see how fine and pretty she is, all that talk'll dry up like the creek in August."

"That's a mighty generous invitation, but I'll have to talk to her about it." It would be suicide and I knew it, at least as far as our time in this place was concerned. Aside from that, I really just didn't have the energy to move on from this place just yet. It was always really hard to pack up and escape in the middle of the night, then find a new place, try to settle in and find a new job. It was hard to pick up any work that wasn't manual labor in a situation like that, and I'm not sure how much more of it my body could take. I was constantly aching with a dull pain in all of my joints.

"If she's agreeable, we'll be down here dancin', hootin' and hollerin' all night."

"Much obliged for your invitation."

With that, I tipped my hat politely and walked slowly up the staircase, wondering if I'd even tell Sylvia of the gracious but impossible invitation.

Sylvia had been staring out the window, teasing out her hair with her favorite boar bristle brush. She was completely hypnotized by the haunting view from our second story picture window.

It was the shambles of the old city. Most of the towns left these days were established in the desolate perimeter of the old places.

The old places were garbage-strewn wastelands. The skyscrapers we could see had no windows, giving the city all the appearance of a broad smile full of rotted and missing teeth. No matter how many times I laid eyes on it with the light of the setting sun behind it, it made me sick to think that all of that destruction could happen all over again.

How it all happened is a very long story. The short version is that Sylvia's kind was responsible for it, though there aren't many of her kind left to blame for it. My heart grew heavy watching her there, standing against that horizon, looking out over the destruction her kind had caused.

Softly, I called her name, bringing her back from the cold past and into the danger of the here and now.

"Sylvia."

She turned, adding a smile to her face, almost as an afterthought in deference to me.

"Darling."

Her face brightened, she dropped her brush, and we met in the center of the room in a tight embrace. Our love was forbidden and our daily embrace after my return home from work was something out of a cheap book. It rang so true though, that no matter how clichéd it was, it made sense for us. I was her only contact with the outside world. I alone understood her, and I alone loved her. After what her kind did to ours, some could wonder how possible it could be that I loved her so deeply, but you'd just have to see her and know her like I do.

She's soft and delicate with a thick head of brunette hair and alabaster skin. Her curves lead you along gently like a scenic, winding road, and she smelled constantly of lilac.

What happened wasn't her fault, but folks in this world have a hard time seeing past that.

I spent time kissing every pale freckle on her tender shoulders before we sat to talk, nose to nose as lovers do.

"It's started, my love. Folks are talkin'."

"Let them. Talk never hurts us."

"Talkin' leads to hurtin', and I'd die if they hurt you."

She smiled sadly and ran her fingers through my hair and then down ever so lightly across my neck.

It gave me a shiver.

"The fella downstairs, Mr. Witwer, wants us to come down to the town social tonight. He says it'll stop all the talking."

"Will it?"

"No. It'll make it worse. He's bein' friendly enough, he just doesn't know you're..."

I hung my head, unable to say it out loud.

"You can say it, go ahead."

"I don't even want to think it. It doesn't matter. You're all I want, what you are is beside the point."

"It makes me smile, seeing you so in love with me." Her eyes locked with mine. She smiled again and kissed my lips.

"I love you," I whispered.

"I know you think it's a bad idea, but can we?"

"Can we what?"

"Can we go? I love you, and you're my everything, but you don't understand how hard it is being locked up here all by myself all the time. I feel like a prisoner."

"Oh, sweetheart. You're not a prisoner. It's just dangerous. If folks found out about us, we'd have to start over all over again."

"I know. But I can't live like this all the time."

My hand crept up her blouse, slowly against the delicate skin of her stomach. "You'll die any other way."

Her other hand pulled up the back of my shirt. The feeling of her palm against the flesh of my back sent a comforting jolt coursing through my body.

We kissed and kissed again. My hand reached up further, cupping her chest.

"Maybe me being dead would be better for you."

"Shhh. Don't even think that."

Our voices had grown more and more hushed as our advances on each other had grown more aggressive. Our worries grew small and disappeared as quickly as our conversation did with the onset of our lovemaking.

Sylvia was always a gentle and passionate lover for the most part, but she always seemed to grow claws that would leave deep, red tracks on my body at the height of her climaxing. The sting made me feel alive.

Afterwards, I flopped down onto my back, fanning the sweat on my face, struggling to breath at a normal rate.

Sylvia stood up, putting herself back together, sweat glistening on her naked body. As she pinned her hair up into a high bun, she looked down at me and smiled coyly. "Let's do it anyway."

"We just did."

"No. Let's go downstairs."

"You know that's crazy."

"What's wrong with being crazy once in a while? I'm going crazy cooped up in here all the time anyway. I need to see people."

"Aren't I enough for you?"

"You are. You're everything I need in a man. But I need people, too. And fun and adventure. More than anything I need to dance. Will there be dancing?

"I expect."

"Then we have to go. It's not like they can tell anything just by looking at me. It always takes a little more than that to catch on and we won't be down there long enough for that. One dance and that's all."

"You never know, love. There's folk who can tell one of your kind a mile away just by looking at you."

"How?"

"I don't know. Instinct or something. Same reason folks like you spook animals sometimes."

"I want to risk it. For one dance. What's the worst that could happen? We'd have to leave again?"

"A lot worse could happen than that."

"We'll see, won't we?"

This was not a good idea.

In the back corner of the saloon was an acoustic three-piece band accompanied by an old ragtime piano. It gave the whole place the sort of feeling you'd get in one of those western movies they made in the old times.

The whole town was there, most of them were congregating in the center of the room, dancing and carrying on. There were some card games in the corner opposite the music men, and the bar was packed from one end to the other. I don't think I'd ever seen Mr. Witwer's place so jumping with life.

I was hoping to be inconspicuous, but Sylvia held everyone's attention with each and every step down the grand staircase. She was every bit as radiant as the first time I saw her and I could feel the eyes of every other man in the room beaming right at her.

If there's one thing those that made her did right, it was that they made them as beautiful as her.

It wasn't long before we found ourselves in the middle of the dance floor. Sylvia had whispered into my ear her deep insistence that I dance with her and who was I to refuse? I was no dancer, and to be honest, the thought of moving slow in time with Sylvia in front of all these people made my stomach turn just a little bit. I was never a dancer and never fancied it. The only kind of dancing I liked was when I was alone with Sylvia and we could press ourselves up close to each other, close our eyes, and sway to the music in our hearts. It didn't feel as pure in front of people, like it was for show, and that part of it always turned my stomach just a little bit. But this is what she wanted, and making her happy is always what made me most happy.

We pressed up against each other like we were alone, upstairs, and hidden from prying eyes. I lost myself in the swaying, pretending as hard as I could that we weren't surrounded by all these townsfolk.

It was hard to shut them all out knowing full well that if they knew what I knew about the woman in my arms, they'd at the very least do their best to try to kill us. I tried even harder to put the heat and sting of all the proverbial torches and pitchforks I'd almost been ended by in the last three years out of my mind as well.

I took in a deep breath of her perfume from the back of her neck, relocating the thoughts in my head to her and the here and now. It was then that I noticed that the music the band was playing was much too fast for our slow dance. *Always to the beat of our own drum,* I thought. *My God, how I love her.*

Either she read my mind or I must have accidentally said that last part out loud because she lifted herself up and brought her lips up to my ear, brushing them against it as she whispered gently, "I love you, too."

We danced right through another pair of up-tempo pieces before I grew tired. "I need a drink."

She kissed my cheek, "I'll be right here. There's still a dance or two left in me."

The bar was friendly and inviting. I ordered a tall, cool draught of beer and turned, sipping into the foamy head before peering at my Sylvia, alone in the center of the dance floor.

Alone, she kept better time with the music, moving back and forth with the beat. It wasn't long before she caught the eye of one of the young men in the crowd. He bowed his head politely and I could tell he'd asked her for a dance. Her eyes met mine from across the room; she could feel my worry. Letting people close to her was not something I did lightly, but in this case it might seem more suspicious to not let them dance. It was a bad idea, but causing a fuss would be worse. Sure, maybe I'd be mistaken for a jealous lover, but it wouldn't take much to add two and two together with me hiding her up in her room all the time.

Hesitantly, I nodded to her, giving her the okay, and she bowed and graciously accepted his invitation. The music began again, a slow number this time. They danced as close as he felt like he could get away with, their stance was quite formal and the dancing rigid. I tried my hardest to swallow all of the bad feelings that go along with watching another man dance with your lady. It was just a dance, but it still worried me and set off all the base instincts of the beasts us civilized folk work so hard to repress.

You can imagine my infuriated confusion when the music ended and she leaned in, right close to his ear and seemed to kiss him on the cheek and whisper something in his ear. I about boiled over before I realized that all the girls seemed to be doing it and she must have just been thanking him. I quickly knew she must have told him much more than that when he shoved her hands off of him, disgusted with something. It didn't even register. I took another draught of my beer.

I thought nothing of it, she smiled at me, just standing there, waiting for something.

It wasn't until I noticed that the beau she'd danced with had whispered into the ears of a pair of his mates, and they turned to whisper to their mates, that I realized that a commotion was being made. The moment they laid a hand on her, I slammed my beer down, and made a move to intervene, but I was across the room and word of what she was had clearly spread like wild fire.

I shouted my entreaties, but they fell on deaf ears. No one cared. She was responsible and the law was clear. They lifted her up into the crowd but she was completely calm. In fact, I was confident she was smiling right at me.

Six of them it took to keep me from rescuing her. Six of them to pull me back and hold me down through all of my thrashing. I'm sure I damaged more than a couple of them pretty bad, I wasn't above biting, and scratching, and tearing, and pulling. It was always my philosophy that anything worth fighting for was worth fighting dirty for. And Sylvia was the most precious thing in my life. If I had the means and the strength I'd've fought a hundred men. But those six foiled me.

"Leave her alone..."

"Shut it, you damned collaborator."

"I'm not--"

--a meaty fist shut my mouth for me and everything went black.

I awoke some hours later.

Alone.

On the outskirts of town.

From there I could see beyond the saloon we'd lived in and into the town square where they'd hung her from the neck until dead. That was the sentence for anyone of her kind found after the purge.

My heart broke. Replicant or not, I loved her and all I could feel were hot tears on my face and sadness in my stomach.

After a while, I rose from my prostrate position. The tears still came, but I didn't notice them as much. I spent a time swaying in the breeze like a dead tree, wondering if I could get to her and cut her down before they cut me down. It wasn't likely, but I wasn't going anywhere without her.

One foot in front of the other.

That's the way things always started, that's the way they end.

Each step that brought me closer to her beautiful, lifeless body made me wonder why she did this.

Was it too much for her?

Was she doing it for me?

I'll never know her mind on this world.

May as well find out in the next one.

The Flights of Angels

Once upon a time there was a little boy named Peter. He was a cherubic young man with rosy cheeks and an easy smile, but no smile of his was ever greater or more full of love than the one he saved for his mother and father. When Peter was in his ninth year, he grew very sick, and it concerned his parents very much because, you see, he was the dearest thing in their lives. It was his broad, loving smile that set warmth and joy in their hearts.

But Peter was in bed with a fever for many weeks and no matter how often he told his mother that he would be all right, she would still break down into tears just outside of his bedroom, not realizing he could hear her sadness. Because he was so young, he didn't understand fully that his mothers tears came not from something bad he'd done, but because she was grief-stricken by the idea she would lose her precious little boy. It always seemed to get worse after the doctor would come to pay a visit.

"Peter, can you open your mouth wide?" He would ask, peering deep into his throat before stuffing a thermometer inside.

"Take deep breaths now, Peter," he would say as he listened to Peter's breathing. Peter would take as many deep breaths as he could before bursting out into a deep, moist cough.

"Just relax now, Peter," he would say as he felt the glands in Peter's neck and stomach with rough but gentle fingers.

Whenever he finished his examination, he would always tousle young Peter's hair and laugh, hiding a grim smile on his face.

Peter would stare longingly out the window while the doctor offered his report to Peter's parents. Outside Peter's window was the swing his father built for him on the tree in the yard. Perhaps the most fun he'd ever had in his life that he could remember was the day his father put the swing up. It was a cool, clear autumn a year past. The leaves on the tree had mostly dropped to the ground and Peter busily raked them into one giant pile while his father strung up the seat made of a scrap of discarded oak onto a sturdy branch. Anyone within a mile could hear little but their laughter for hours. Peter's father would push him higher and higher until Peter was high enough to jump headlong into the pile of leaves, scattering them back over the yard. With the help of his father, Peter would rake the leaves back up as fast as he could, trying hard to get in as many flights as possible before the sun fell and he'd be sent to bed.

Now, though, it was winter and the tree was bare-limbed and cold, dusted with snow.

Peter could not hear what the doctor told his mother, but he knew things must be bad from his concerned murmur. What told him the most, however, was the sharp, stifled cry his mother let out after the doctor finished his prognosis.

It was then that young Peter decided that he would work hard to get better and to smile his great, big, loving smile for his mother as much as he could.

But those weeks were short, and on Monday the seventeenth, Peter went to sleep for the last time.

His mother had kissed him on the forehead and his father had read him a story before he fell asleep that night, and he had one final, fevered dream eternal.

"What would you like, Peter?" A voice asked him.

"I'd like to play," Peter said. "I've been in bed a long time and I miss playing so much."

"Then you shall play," the voice said and the blackness gave way to a playground of a size and like such as Peter had never seen. And feeling fit and eager to play, Peter raced about, spinning on the merry-go-round, careening down the slide, swinging on the swings, and clambering up and down the jungle gyms. But soon he became tired. Playing by himself was quite exhausting and quickly grew lonesome.

As he thought this, he turned to see a young boy, about his age and dressed in pajamas, staring at the park, eager to play. So long had it been for Peter to have a playmate of any kind that he smiled and went over to the boy as quickly as his legs could carry him. Peter put his arm around the boy and shook his hand all at the same time. "I'm Peter. Isn't this park great? What's your name?"

"I'm John."

"Hello, John."

And that was it. They formed the sort of fast friendship that only children are capable of. For what felt like hours they played and laughed. They laughed and played almost as hard as Peter and his father on that autumn day in the past. The only difference was this was missing the blanket of warmth and care that only a loving parent can provide. Their fun was quickly cut short, though, when a voice called John away. "It's time to move on," the voice said.

"I guess I have to go," John told Peter.

A sad appreciation crept over Peter, and he gave John a hug and thanked him for playing.

Peter stared solemnly into the bright distance, waving farewell to John on his way into the beyond.

"Goodbye, John!" He shouted after him.

“Goodbye, Peter!” John shouted back.

Soon, John was only a speck in the distance.

Peter didn't have long to mourn the departure of his new friend before a voice called out from behind him, across the green. "He-ey!"

"Hello!" Peter shouted back.

The two boys ran toward each other, finally meeting by the merry-go-round. Both boys were winded badly.

"I'm Michael," the new little boy said between heavy breaths. "What's your name?"

"Peter."

"How do you do, Peter?"

"I'm fine."

"Where are we?"

"A park, I think, but I don't know where."

"How'd we get here?"

"I don't know. I'm sure it's a dream. The last thing I remember before I got here was my father reading me a bedtime story. I was very sick then, though, and now I'm better."

"I was walking in the woods with my brother and I lost him. It seems like I've been walking for ages, but I finally came upon this place."

"Hmmm..."

"Are there any adults here?"

"I haven't seen any."

"I hope."

"Me too, but I think there's really only one thing to do until they find us."

"What's that?"

"Tag! You're it!"

With a laugh, Peter chased after Michael; back and forth their game went. Hours passed. They chased each other around trees and rocks like dogs chasing their own tails. The wonderful sound of children playing echoed in the ether for miles around until a voice interrupted the merriment, this time to call Michael away.

Once again, Peter felt an overwhelming compulsion to embrace his playmate and whisper to him quietly how much he appreciated their time together. Michael walked off into the distance, turning periodically to wave back at Peter, showing him how appreciated he felt during their brief time together.

Though his friend was leaving, Peter took heart, knowing he was able to make him feel welcome and wanted. Nothing made Peter more sad than the feeling that there were people in the world who didn't have love and care, people who appreciated them. Then Peter tried to imagine what it would be like to be lost, separated from his family the way Michael had been. He tried hard to empathize, but he simply couldn't wrap his head around it. Trying too hard to fathom that sense of abandonment made his brain spin about like the merry-go-round he was sitting on. Peter liked feeling comforted and loved, and took pride in trying to make others feel that way, and so it was with great delight that Peter noticed a young girl walking toward him from the same direction his other recent friends had come from.

She was a few years older than Peter and had dark hair in wavy curls that brushed along the back of her neck. Her smile was wide and bright, like an angel would smile. She reminded Peter of his mother, and it made him shed a tear as he wondered where his mother was.

But the young girl saw his trembling chin and red eyes and when she arrived, she kneeled down and delicately wiped the tears from little Peter's face. "Shhh," she soothed, "what's your name?"

Trying to hold back a flood of tears, Peter's chin quivered when he told her his name, but once he spoke he sobbed and the tears flowed freely.

"There, there," she ran her fingers across his head, trying to comfort him. "What's the matter, Peter?"

The fact that he was forced to form the words choked him up and his tears doubled in force, cutting him off.

"It's okay, dear heart. Shhh... You don't need to cry. You can tell me what's the matter."

"I miss my mother," Peter was finally able to say. "...and my father...and I don't know where I am."

"It's all right. We're together now. I don't exactly know where we are either, but I'm sure we can find your parents." She pulled Peter close to her, embracing him, soothing him as best she could.

He let it all out, crying until he could suppress it. He pulled away from her, sat up, and wiped his eyes and nose on his sleeve.

"I don't know where we are. I think this is a nightmare."

"What makes you say that?"

"I was sleeping before. And now I'm here. And it was fun for a while. But I want to wake up and be home."

"Well, why don't we see if there's a way we can wake up? I'd very much like to be home, too."

Peter nodded his head to the girl. She stood and offered him her hand, to help him up. He accepted it. All he could think of was how wonderful her soft, cool hands felt pressed against his skin, comforting somehow, like holding his mothers hand.

"What's your name?" he asked the girl leading him toward the edge of the park.

"My name is Wendy," she said.

"I'm sorry I cried like that, Wendy."

"You don't ever have to be sorry about missing your family, Peter."

They walked and walked for what felt like miles, until they arrived at a stony precipice that looked down hundreds of feet into a deep ravine. A chill ran up Peter's spine.

"What do you think?" Wendy asked him.

"What do you mean?"

"I mean, let's do it."

"Do what?"

"Don't you love the feeling of falling in dreams, knowing you'll be safe when you hit the ground?"

Peter wasn't sure what to think when she closed her eyes and took a step closer to the edge, but the overwhelming sensation that he had nothing to lose washed over him and he followed her lead.

"One," she counted. "Two."

There was a long, terrible pause before she said, "Three."

Neither hesitated to leap off the cliff.

The wind sailed through their hair as they fell and fell and fell. And the rush they felt was exactly the same as when you fall in a dream. It's disconcerting but wonderful all at the same time. But instead of hitting the ground at the bottom of the ravine in a horrible splat, they continued flying through the air as though it were as natural as walking or breathing.

Still led by Wendy and her hand, Peter soared back to the top of the ravine, hovering over its middle.

"That didn't wake us up, did it?"

"No, but it was fun, wasn't it?"

"Let's do it again!"

And they zoomed around in the air like birds in spring. More than a few times they came down to the water below and flew over it, reaching down into it, skimming the surface with their hands.

The whole time, they never let go of each other.

After a time, they flew back up to the top of the precipice and sat down, looking over the edge. This filled Peter with an anxiety. Each of his playmates had been taken from him after their playtime and he didn't want to lose Wendy to the voice and he told her so.

"I'll be right here," she assured him.

She began to sing him a lullaby, very similar to the one his mother used to sing to him and he curled up next her with his head in her lap. Her voice was so relaxing to him that he drifted off into a restful sleep.

When he awoke once more, she was gone.

Panic struck him.

Where could she have gone? Did she wake up from the dream? Was that even possible?

The thing Peter hated the most was that he wasn't able to say goodbye to her, that he couldn't tell her how much he appreciated her comfort. If he was going to be here, he thought, and have to walk with these other lost children, the least he could do is make them feel not so lonely on their way.

He resolved at that moment to make sure every lost boy and girl who crossed his path would be met with as much comfort and fun and love as he could muster until he could find a way out of this dream and back into the loving arms of his parents.

And that was what he did.

Hundreds of children arrived at the park through hundreds of sleepless days and Peter made sure that every young boy or girl left to the other side with a hug and the knowledge that even though they didn't have very much time, they were loved, cared for, and wanted. There was nothing more sad, in his mind, than someone leaving his presence without feeling important and cherished.

But soon this burden grew too much for young Peter.

Where was his comfort?

The feeling he had worked so hard to prevent in all the other children soon began to eat away at him and he spent much of his free time building up the courage to finally ask the voice what his purpose was. Why was he left here? Did no one want him after all?

"Perhaps my parents wanted to leave me here," he told himself. And that thought made him cry. What did he do wrong? What could he have done to deserve such abandonment?

The gears in his mind worked overtime trying to understand why he was so unwanted by everyone. Every time another child would come through his park (and he had begun to think of it as his, since he was the only constant there) he would shower them with all the attention and affection to feel warm and loved, but it would never be enough for them to stay with him. The voice would always call them away and they would always leave Peter, alone and discarded.

And it made him cry.

There is nothing sadder than a child (or anyone) crying because no one wants them.

One day, after a long hard day of showing a wonderful time and an unheard of amount of care to a little boy named James, the voice once more called away Peter's playmate.

"Won't you stay here with me, James?" Peter asked as he latched onto him with both arms, hoping his new friend would show him the same respect given him.

"He cannot stay, Peter," the voice replied for James.

"I'd like to," James offered, "but I guess I really have to go."

James started off on his walk beyond, leaving Peter alone and unwanted once more.

"Why can't he stay?" Peter asked through bitter tears.

"Because it is his time to go."

"When is it my time?"

"That's not up to me, Peter."

"I want to leave here."

"Is that what you want?"

"Yes! I want to go back home. I want to wake up, I want to grow up and be a normal kid! I want someone to love me..."

The voice made no reply.

"Can I?" Peter asked.

But still no reply came. And Peter was even more alone and left feeling twice as unwanted and rejected as before.

And that's when he got up, smudged the hot tears away from his eyes and moved forward in the same direction James and John and Michael had left him for. He walked with a fire and determination that was out of character for so gentle a boy. He practically marched. And soon the march wasn't enough and he galloped, hoping to come to the end of this place and somewhere he could be with people who loved him again. Perhaps he could find someone to replace his parents since they obviously didn't want him anymore.

Farther and farther he went until finally he came upon something he'd never seen before in all of his time there. It was a house, much like his own house, the one he lived in before all this. In the front was a mighty tree very similar to the one his father had put the swing in.

Peter's heart grew faint. Could this have been his house?

He doubted it. Nothing in his dream (which is what he came to think of it as) ever turned out to be what it seemed. But at the same time, his mind was spinning with the possibilities.

He raced to the front door of the imposing house and knocked heavily on it, hoping someone, anyone, was home. He was prepared to ask the inhabitants to take him, they didn't need to do much, just love him. That's all he needed. That's all any child needed: to be loved.

The door creaked open and a woman opened the door, a woman ten years older than his mother was, at least. But when he smiled his beautiful smile, he was happy that an adult was here, happy that they might have answers, happy that they might be convinced to love him. The woman shrieked.

"Peter?" she asked.

How did she know his name unless she knew him?

The door opened wider and Peter could see a figure on an arm-chair through the banister. Soft yellow light poured in and the man sitting in the chair looked up and it was unmistakably Peter's father. He looked up from his paper at the mention of Peter's name to see his little boy, back to normal; happy and smiling like the sweet, bright boy he was because for the first time in ages Peter no longer felt he was living in a nightmare.

He stood and adjusted his glasses to be sure the sight before him was no illusion. And looking into the face of that beautiful, little boy, that he cherished more than anything else in the world, he knew finally that he was in heaven.

7092736R00110

Made in the USA
San Bernardino, CA
27 December 2013